Seduced by the Blues

A Fox Cove Mystery

Michelle Lorette

MLH
CRAFTS

For my family— you get me, and even when you don't, you accept me.
Thank you.

CHAPTER ONE

LIFE SUCKS.

The chirping of the microwave broke through my brain fog, bringing me back into the present, into the apartment I shared with my roommate, Lilli. I turned away from the window I had been staring out of, away from the view of the small backyard and the cars parked behind it. I hadn't really been noticing any of it anyway.

I shuffled over and opened the microwave door, taking out my coffee mug filled with warmed creamer, then poured hot coffee from the pot that had been set the night before to brew at 6 AM. I sighed as I sat down at the little two-seat counter and let the steam from the coffee drift over my face as I closed my eyes. That's how Lilli found me when she walked in a few minutes later.

"You're up early," she said as she reached for a coffee mug. "If I were you, I'd be sleeping in."

"And if I were you, I'd still have a job," I couldn't quite keep the sarcasm out of my voice. I opened my eyes and met her sleepy gaze.

She squinted her eyes at me as she took her flavored creamer out of the fridge, heated it, and mixed it in her coffee.

She didn't say anything else, just frowned as she fixed her coffee, put the creamer back, then came and sat next to me. We sat there, sipping coffee until she set hers down on the counter and turned to me.

"It sucks, I know," she said as if she had read my mind from moments ago. She forced me to set my coffee mug down. She grabbed my hands and squeezed them gently, making me look at her. "I really do know, De. I was laid off in my first year out of college. Budget cuts, they suck."

"Yep," I said, "and they suck even more when you're almost thirty. But I'm OK, Lilli, or at least I will be. Just let me wallow for a little while."

"Uh-uh, you wallowed all weekend, and Monday, and Tuesday. It's a bad habit with you, and as your best friend, I'm shutting it down. It's time to update your resume, update your LinkedIn profile, and update your hair style for goodness sake. This horse tail braid has got to go," she said, smiling as she tugged on my hair.

"Ow, that *is* attached to my head! What's wrong with my braid?" I whined.

"Nothing, if you're going to head out west and take up ranching," she teased. "But come on, Deana, don't you think it's time to let this go? If you want long hair, that's fine, but all you do is put it up in a ponytail or braid."

"Well, that's easier to work with," I whined.

"Don't play dumb. You know what I mean, and you know I'm right." She grabbed her mug and headed out of the kitchen and back to her room. I made a face at her back and frowned as I sipped my coffee and went back to staring into space.

"I saw that!" Lilli shot back before she shut her bedroom door.

I knew she was right, at least about my moping. I had to stop feeling sorry for myself. Yes, it sucked that after almost six years working with the Philadelphia Library Cooperative, I had been laid off due to budget cuts and branch mergers. And it wasn't great that it had happened just as I was thinking that I had gained enough experience, as first a library assistant and then a cataloger, that I could begin applying for a management position. But technically, I guess I was still in my twenties, even if it was only for three more months, and the twenties were about growth and finding yourself, right? So technically, I still had three months to get my life together again.

I groaned as I put my head in my hands. Who was I kidding? I was thirty, almost, and jobless.

This sucked.

AFTER LILLI LEFT FOR work, I finally took a shower and got dressed. I had been living in my pjs and sweats for four days. I supposed it was time for real clothes. I decided to try clearing my head with a little old-fashioned exercise, so I grabbed my bike from the shed in the backyard.

Thankfully, it was a cool but sunny day. Spring in Pennsylvania could be anywhere between freezing temps with snow to mid-80s with sunny days and humidity. Most of the trees in the neighborhood were looking hopeful that the weather would stay warm. The dogwoods that I rode past had blooms covering their limbs and the oaks and maples and other trees that I didn't know the names of had small leaves beginning to fill in along their branches. It felt good to feel my legs moving with the bike pedals, the breeze feathering the loose bits of my hair, and the bright sunshine warming my back. By the time I got to the section of the bike trail near Mt. Moriah Cemetery I almost felt like smiling.

After I finished my ride, I walked my bike back up along Brick Street. The shops, boutiques, bars, and cafes catered mostly to locals but were eclectic enough that they drew a fair amount of tourists as well. I was just passing the window of Lacy's Salon when I looked in and caught the eye of the woman at the front desk. She was on the phone but smiled and waved at me. I waved back and kept walking, but then stopped. I fingered my braid, which had gotten a little messy from my bike ride, and then before I could talk myself out of it, I locked my bike to the closest bike rack, walked back and opened the salon door.

"Hi. Welcome to Lacy's," the same woman I had seen from outside said to me. She was off the phone now and gave me the same friendly smile. "Do you have an appointment?"

"No. Are you taking walk-ins?" I asked. I didn't know if I was hoping she'd say yes or no. If she said no then I could just leave and tell myself I had tried, but obviously wasn't meant to get a haircut. If she said yes, then what? My entire life would change — because of a haircut?

"Of course," she said, still smiling. "If you take a seat I'll see who's available. It might be a few minutes." She looked down at what I assumed was a schedule book in front of her on the desk, then typed a few keys on the computer keyboard.

"Melissa will be able to see you in about five minutes," she said as the phone rang. She took the call, then a minute later said, "I'll take you back and get your hair washed now. Are you ready?"

"OK," I said, getting back up.

"It looks like you've been out bike riding," she said as she got me seated at the wash bowl, placed a towel around my neck, and tipped my head back."

"Yes, it seemed like a good day for it."

"I haven't been on a bike in ages. My boyfriend and I used to ride all of the time. We stopped after he hurt his knee. It's always the knees that get messed up, have you noticed?"

She continued talking about her boyfriend's knee injury, their holiday trip they were planning to take, and her present nursing studies. I mostly listened, interjecting a few times if she asked me a question, but not really sharing very much. I've never been good at small talk. It's probably why I prefer reading a book to sitting with friends in a bar or restaurant — or maybe reading the book is why I'm not good at small talk?

An hour later I walked out of the salon with a shorter head of hair and a bag of styling products. Andrea, the very friendly front desk-hair washer had talked me into a hot oil treatment after seeing the number of split ends I possessed, then had talked me into buying a couple of treatment packs to use at home. As I left the salon, I stuck the salon bag into the small backpack I had brought with me, collected my bike from the bike rack, and headed home.

Lilli found me in the kitchen when she got home from work. I was pulling wine and cheese out of the fridge, so she didn't actually see me until I closed the door. She was talking on her cell. From her side of the conversation, it sounded to me like it was her sister, Rose, on the phone. As she saw me she screamed and ran the rest of the way towards me.

"Oh my God! You look amazing!" she yelled, picking up the ends of my newly styled hair. After the hair stylist, Melissa, talked to me about what I wanted, she unwound my braid and then cut six inches off the end. Once she was sure I wasn't going to run screaming from the salon she continued, checking with me before each additional cut of the length. The end result was a haircut that came just below my shoulders, with enough length to still put up in a ponytail or twist, maybe even a very short braid. I had been playing with the ends and swinging my hair back and forth since I got home, surprised by how much lighter the weight of it felt and how freely it swung whenever I moved.

"What? No, we're fine," Lilli said into her phone, "but you should see De. She got a haircut! What? Oh, that's a great idea. OK, I'll let you know." She hung up, looked at me again and then gave me a hug, holding out the hair on the sides of my head. "I'm so proud of you," she said. "This is such a huge step for you."

"It's just a haircut, Lilli," I said, downplaying what had been an emotional experience for me and swatting her hand away as she tried to grab my hair again.

I poured two glasses of wine and then started slicing the cheese I had set out on the cheese board. Lilli took one of the glasses and handed me the other, making me set aside the slicer.

"To Deana Weber, her new hair, and her new life. May it take her far and teach her much. And may her hair never reach her butt again." She held up her glass and tipped it until it clinked against mine.

"Cheers," I said as I laughed. "You're a little nuts."

"All the best psychologists are," she responded and then took a drink.

I finished slicing cheese, put it away and took out a few slices of prosciutto, rolling and adding them to the cheese board. Lilli grabbed a jar of olives and then she and I sat at the counter with our wine and ate. Some evenings if we ate together we chose snack meals like this instead of a full meal. Other times we pulled out milk and cereal, or just bypassed it all and went for a pint of ice cream.

"Was that Rose on the phone?" I asked.

"Uh-huh," Lilli said as she munched. "She wants us to come over on Friday for a movie night, and maybe shopping on Saturday. We could sleep over if you want. Franklin and the kids are at his parents until Saturday night, so she's excited for some grown-up girls time."

"I'll check my schedule," I said sarcastically.

Lilli chuckled. "Sarcasm, huh, must be the next emotional phase after wallowing."

"Is that your clinical opinion, Doctor?"

"Yes, I'm completing a study. I'm calling it The Pre-Midlife Crisis Anomaly."

By Friday I had managed to update my resume and networking profile and had even cleaned out my closet a little. I had two bags of gently used clothes to drop off at the second hand store, plus another full trash bag of old makeup, magazines, and worn out shoes that was on its way to the dump. Lilli had talked me into the movie night with her twin sister, Rose, followed by brunch and shopping on Saturday. Rose was an elementary teacher with two kids, a husband and a cat. She had one of those idyllic lives in the city suburbs that Lilli and I equally made fun of and also secretly envied.

We got to Rose's just as her husband, Franklin, was driving off with the kids. We waved to him and walked into the house. Rose was mixing sangria in the kitchen. She already had a huge bowl of popcorn made.

"Hello, hello," Lilli sung as we walked in.

"Oh, thank God you're here," Rose sighed. "I have needed some time off from kids for weeks. This pitcher was looking very good. If you hadn't shown up I would have given serious thought to drinking it all myself."

"We can't have that," Lilli teased. "I'd have to call mom and dad and explain to them that their daughter is a lush."

"As if," Rose shot back. "We both know who the wino is in this family."

Lilli stuck her tongue out at her sister, then motioned to the wine glasses on the counter. "Just start pouring."

Rose poured and handed each of us a glass. Lilli grabbed the bowl of popcorn that Rose had made and started walking into the family room. "Let's get this party started," she called back. "What are we watching?"

"I'm in the mood for a sappy romance," Rose said as we followed Lilli, "or maybe a mystery, but it still has to have some romance as well."

"So the choices are sappy romance or mystery romance," Lilli mused. "I'm sensing a theme. Is Franklin not fulfilling his husbandly duties?"

"Franklin is doing fine." Rose said as she sat in the middle of the couch. "We don't have a lot of couple time these days, though."

"So let me take the kids for a little bit," Lilli offered. "Isn't that what intelligent, successful aunts are for?"

Rose snorted. "You think you could handle Becca and Matthew, by yourself?"

"Of course. They love their Auntie Lil. How about next weekend? You and Franklin plan a date night and I'll clear my schedule."

"That would be really great, Lilli. And when you finally settle down and have kids, I'll pay you back."

"I've gotta find a guy first, dear sister."

"Not necessarily," I said.

"Oh no. If I'm having a baby, I'm going to have all of the old-fashioned hanky-panky first, and a lot of it." Lilli smirked as she sipped her sangria.

"I've missed this," Rose said as she smiled at us.

"Good," Lilli said decisively. "Now let's pick a movie. I vote for mystery. What about you, Deana?"

"Definitely mystery," I agreed. "I don't think I could handle sappy right now."

I settled into the couch cushions beside Rose. She set up the movie just as Lilli plopped down on her other side. Lilli handed her the bowl of popcorn, which I immediately stuck my hand in and grabbed a fistful of.

"Hey," Rose whined, "Why am I holding the popcorn bowl?"

"Cause you're in the middle, sis," Lilli said.

"Well, this isn't happening. Go get a few bowls for us to hold."

"But I'll miss the beginning of the movie," Lilli whined back.

I smiled at them both as I munched on popcorn. I had two younger brothers, Lance and Phillip, but they were closer to each other in age, so I was usually their baby sitter or referee. Watching Lilli and Rose argue made me miss them, and also made me a little envious that they had each other.

Lilli came back in with bowls. She tousled Rose's hair as she reached over and passed me one. They both had the quintessential Irish freckles and red hair, though Rose's had highlights and was a shorter pixie cut. She threw some popcorn at her sister, which Lilli caught a piece of and popped in her mouth, giving Rose a smug look as she sat back down.

Twenty minutes from the end of the movie, my phone vibrated. I looked over at the screen as it sat on the side table at the end of the couch. My mom's picture popped up in the center of the screen. I wondered what she could want on a Friday night, but decided to wait and call her back once the movie was over. I sent a quick text to let her know so she wouldn't keep calling.

We took a couple of breaks for bathroom runs and topping up our sangria. By the time the movie was over it was after eleven. I realized it was too late to call my mom back. I'd have to do it in the morning.

CHAPTER TWO

I WAS UP BEFORE LILLI and Rose Saturday morning. I quietly set up the coffee maker and heated some cream, making an effort not to slam the cabinet doors as I got a mug. I dialed my parents' home phone as I sat curled up in the love seat with my steaming caramel latte. My mom and dad were old school enough that they still paid for a land line in their home. As the phone rang, I imagined mom and dad sitting at the glass top table in the breakfast nook. Any time I was home visiting, Saturdays would start with stove-top oatmeal with fresh blueberries, coffee, and music playing from the retro stereo that dad had gotten as a retirement gift from the police department back in Hickory, North Carolina. I had spent the first twenty years of my life there, moving away the first time to finish my undergrad in Raleigh, then again when I went to grad school and took the job here, in Philadelphia.

My dad had retired eight years ago from the department. I was still in college at the time. He and my mom decided to move to the coast along with my two younger brothers so my dad could pursue his love of fishing by becoming a charter boat captain. They both seemed happy enough living in Wilmington. Since I had already moved out and my brothers would be doing the same soon, they felt like it was a good time to downsize. Their three-bedroom-bungalow style house was comfortably cozy at barely 1,800 square feet. My youngest brother, Phillip, had finished high school the year before my dad retired. He and Lance had shared the second bedroom in Wilmington where they both started college. They had moved out by their second year and now shared an apartment nearby. Phillip had joined the army, after being in ROTC during college, and was now deployed most of the time. Lance had decided he didn't really like college and had decided to finish at a technical school. He got a structural drafting degree and now works at a building firm near Raleigh that he commutes to.

My mom left her job at the bank in Hickory thinking she would retire and spend more time on hobbies, but instead she got involved in the local community and ended up working part-time at the city offices. She's just one of those people who is naturally a joiner. For some reason that trait did not get shared with her only daughter. Every committee and club that I've ever been involved with could be counted on one hand. I didn't even join Girl Scouts.

"Good morning, Mom," I said smiling as I heard her pick up the phone.

"Oh, Deana, I'm so glad you've finally called," she answered.

"I know," I said, trying to head off the lecture about following through when saying I would do something. "I should have called back last night, but by the time the movie was over it was almost midnight, so I decided to call first thing this morning."

"Well, better late than never, sweetie. And how are Lilli and Rose?"

"They're fine. Rose's husband took their kids to visit his parents for the night, so Rose invited us over for a movie. Then today we're going to have brunch and do some shopping."

"That sounds lovely, dear."

So far into the conversation I had been able to avoid my present jobless state. I knew I'd have to tell my parents sometime, but I wanted more time to figure out my next step first.

"How's fishing going?" I asked cheerfully. Mom had a conflicting relationship with Dad's new job. She loved that he was doing something he enjoyed, but, even after eight years, the smell of fish and boat fuel that followed him home was not something she had gotten used to.

"Your dad's at a tournament this weekend in Florida. He rode down with a few others from his charter boat club. But he's flying back early on Monday because he's got a charter going out Tuesday. Actually, that's why I called you. I need your help with something."

"Really?"

"Yes. Do you remember Aunt Stella?"

"Of course I do, your friend from college. How is she?"

"Not so good, sweetie. She died last week."

"What! Mom, I'm so sorry. What happened?"

"Oh, you know, life. Stella always had a bad heart. She had three surgeries by her early 30s. I guess it just delayed things. She had a heart attack last Tuesday that ended up being too much for her."

"Wow, Mom. I didn't know she had a bad heart. You never said."

"Don't be upset. She didn't like to advertise it and I respected her wishes. It never held her back from living her life how she wanted. You remember her going on that photo safari trip to Africa and that other trip to Turkey when you were in high school?"

I smiled. "Yeah, she brought me back a carved giraffe and a Turkish silk scarf. I still have them packed away somewhere." I thought back to all of the times over the years that Aunt Stella had been there. She was in my memories as far back as I *could* remember. And what I couldn't remember was documented in all of the family photos and videos my parents had. She had always been part of my life. But besides a few holiday cards exchanged while I was in college I hadn't really been in touch with her.

"How are you doing, Mom?"

Oh, I'm okay. I've had my moments." I could hear the sadness in her voice, but besides a few sniffs she seemed to be holding herself together. Mom was emotional, but compared to my dad she was definitely more in control of her emotions. My dad, on the other hand, teared up while watching one of those scenic truck commercials.

"So, what do you need? Do you want me to go to her funeral with you."

"No. Stella's not having one. She didn't want it. She was cremated and since she didn't have family, she had her remains shipped to me so that I could spread her ashes in the ocean. Your dad and I are going to do that next month, on her birthday. Phillip won't be here. He's still deployed until August.

But Lance will be able to come. I'd like you to be here also if you can get time off."

"Oh, um, of course," I stuttered. This was the perfect moment to let Mom know I had been laid off, but I couldn't do it. I scrunched my face and bit my lip. Then decided it would be better to get it over with. I was just taking a breath to come clean when Mom started talking again.

"Just let me know if you can be here. Her birthday is...was on May 23. It's so odd to think of her not being out there somewhere. I keep reaching for the phone to give her a quick call before I remember she's not there."

"Yeah, I feel so bad. I hadn't even talked to her since seeing her at your house that time we were all there for Christmas. When was that?"

"About six years ago. She had just finished moving into her new home and was telling me all the plans she had."

"I barely paid attention."

"You were enjoying yourself. You had just finished your master's and had switched to full time at the library. Believe me, Stella and I both understood. We were both young college grads once too. Plus, you had to rush back to your new job so quickly. We barely had you for Christmas and then you missed the New Years party."

"I know. I did have a lot going on, but I still wish I had spent more time with all of you."

"Stella was very proud of you, Deana, and so are your dad and I. We know how much you care."

"OK, well I've got to go get dressed. The girls should be up soon. We're leaving for brunch in an hour."

"Oh, wait. I haven't told you what I need you to do."

"I thought that was what spreading Aunt Stella's ashes was about?"

"No, that's separate. What I need you to do is go to meet Stella's executor. She's a lawyer who's handling the legal stuff for Stella's estate and needs me or another named beneficiary present to sign off on some things. Her name is Gladys Laine."

"Mom, I..."

"It won't take long, Deana. And it's close enough that you shouldn't need to take more than a day off from work. I know it's asking a lot, but I just can't get away right now. There's a big conference going on here about the city's expansion along the river and there's so much for the planning office to deal with. Would you please do this for me, sweetie?"

I sighed. My mom rarely asked me for anything. I couldn't tell her taking off from work would be too difficult when I didn't even have a job anymore, unless I told her I didn't have a job anymore. I could do this one thing and then later fill her in on my situation, and by then maybe I'd even have a few job interviews set up. I don't know why I didn't just tell her. I was almost thirty. Maybe I knew she'd start wanting to brainstorm about resumes, interviews, and networking and I just didn't feel up for that yet. That's me, ever the procrastinator.

"OK, I'll see what I can do. Just email me the contact information for this person. Where did Aunt Stella live anyway? Was she still in Baltimore?"

"No, for the past six years she was living a couple of hours away from you, in Fox Cove, Pennsylvania.

SATURDAY WITH THE SISTERS turned out to be fun, though I was a little distracted about my upcoming road trip. I shared the news with Lilli and Rose, who both seemed to think the idea of me going out of town to deal with the legal affairs of my Aunt Stella's estate was the perfect idea. Lilli thought the time away would allow me to think about my life and goals without being in the middle of it. Rose seemed to think it would be a little farm-filled, country adventure. I'm not really sure what I thought, except that I had nothing better to do. So, by Sunday I had packed, printed out the email from the executor that had been forwarded to me by my mom with contact information and directions to Fox Cove, then had emailed the woman back myself to let her know I was coming and to set up a meeting time.

Monday morning, I loaded up my car and got on the road. Lilli, bless her heart, had made extra coffee so I had a full thermos, and she had bagged up some of her homemade trail mix for me to munch on. She was on one of her 'healthy bodies equal healthy minds' mantras. I wasn't complaining as long as she was making the goodies.

I headed out of Cobbs Creek along West Chester Pike, then turned north when I got to West Chester and jumped on I-76. As usual for springtime in Pennsylvania, the weather had turned rainy and chilly again. Thankfully I had planned for it and had brought a fleece coat as well as an umbrella. Over six years living in the Keystone state had taught me to be prepared for mercurial weather.

As I drove west out of the Philadelphia suburbs, the concrete, stone, and brick gave way to more and more trees and pastures. I actually liked the rural countryside and small towns.

I had grown up in Hickory, NC, and had been surrounded by the wilderness of the Appalachian hills. It was comfortable for me. But I also loved city life. I loved the energy and almost constant motion of people and commerce that I was surrounded by in Philadelphia. Still, taking a break from it did feel a little good, especially when I felt cut off from that energy by my jobless state.

An hour and a half into the trip my bladder decided it had had enough coffee. Just outside of Carlisle I got off of the highway and pulled into a gas station to stretch and take a bathroom break. As I was leaving, I noticed a farm and feed store across the road. Its parking lot had hanging baskets of flowers, garden decorations, stacks of feed bags, a rainbow array of outdoor chairs and rockers, and small wood and wire cages that looked like over-sized hamster houses. I smiled, thinking of how different life on a farm must be.

My GPS let me know that I had about thirty more minutes until I reached my destination. I had an hour before I was supposed to meet with the lawyer. Gladys Laine had emailed me extra directions to her office where I would be meeting her to sign off on the paperwork for Aunt Stella's estate. Since I had some extra time, I decided to detour through Carlisle just for fun.

Carlisle is a borough west of Harrisburg, on the opposite side of the Susquehanna River. Pennsylvania was kind of an oddball when it came to city government structure. It's one of only four states that refer to themselves as a commonwealth, which is technically no different than a state that calls itself a state. It's just a fancier word. Borough is also just a fancier word for town. I think the word choices are one of the reasons that

I liked living here. The old-style words and areas filled with history gave me the feeling that I could touch the past even while I'm going about my day-to-day life.

As I drove down Hanover Street, I felt myself enjoying the scenery. It was one of those small towns that was making an effort to revitalize its downtown area without losing the charm of the old-style homes and businesses.

I turned onto High Street where it met Hanover and continued driving, running into the area that began the campus of Dickinson College. The creamy greige-toned stone buildings mixed in with more modern structures looked so inviting that I was almost tempted to pull over to stop and walk around on the green spaces, as I was seeing many of the college students do. Instead, I kept driving, but promised myself I'd come back sometime to walk around Carlisle and enjoy more of its sights.

CHAPTER THREE

TWENTY MINUTES LATER I was turning off of Route 11 and heading north. As I crested a small hill, my GPS reminded me that my turn was coming up, though when I got to the road, I seriously doubted the computer's directions, especially since the 'turn' was showing up as a blank area on the GPS screen. Obviously, Google had never mapped this particular part of Pennsylvania. The road barely looked wide enough for two cars. Still, I took the turn, followed the curvy road up and around another hill, and was just about to pull over to check my directions when I looked out the passenger side of the windshield and saw the beginnings of a small village set down below the road I was on.

It was so shocking to see such a quaint little village tucked in and surrounded by farmland and forested hills that I'm sure anyone driving towards me would have seen my mouth hanging wide open.

"Would you look at that," I said out loud to the empty car.

I slowed down as I checked the printout that included the executor's address as well as directions to Fox Cove. Now I knew why Ms. Laine had bothered to include them. The empty space on my GPS wasn't empty at all. I read the instructions.

Take a right off of highway, follow curving road as it slopes up and then down, village comes into view as you come around the

last curve, set down in the valley with the hillside you just drove on above you on the right. The road will run right into town, perpendicular to main street. Turn right to get to the center of town. My office is just past the post office, in the white painted brick building with green trim.

I followed the road just as she had written, getting to Main Street and turning right. There was a restaurant on my left that looked interesting with a few cars parked out front. Next, on my right was a small grocery store called Tresser's Market, followed by a pub called The Fox and Fisher. I saw the post office just past the pub, then a townhouse, and then saw Ms. Laine's building. Hers was the first in a row of three Federal style row houses. Back in Philly some of the row houses were called a trinity, because of their three-story layout as well as in reference to the Catholic trinity — a lecture at the library had taught me that little tidbit.

I turned off Main Street into a parking area behind the buildings. There were spaces designated as residential parking and some that weren't marked. I pulled into an unmarked space, got out of my car, stretching a little as I looked around at the tall hill that flanked this end of the village, then walked back around to the front of the building.

As I stepped into the office I heard a tinkling sound. A few seconds later a cat emerged from somewhere towards the back, most likely the kitchen if this layout followed most row house plans. In England and in earlier building styles the kitchen would have been in the basement, but someone finally realized what a fire hazard that was and moved it up a floor - yep, same lecture. Sometimes I surprised myself with how much unconnected information was rolling around in my head.

THE CAT MADE A CIRCLE around my legs, flicked its tail, and then sauntered back out of the room. At the same time a woman walked in from the same entry. "Hi! It's so nice to meet you, Deana. I'm Gladys Laine," she said happily and a little distractedly as she held out her hand.

"Your aunt Stella was such a sweetheart. She was one of my favorite clients; actually, she was my first, right after I moved here a couple of years ago. She came through the door like a ball of energy, saying that Trini at the Sparrow — that's our cafe in town — mentioned there was a new woman attorney. She decided right then and there that she had to meet me and hire me.

Oh, but you don't need to hear all of this. How was your drive? I'm originally from Cleveland so I know how hectic city traffic can be."

Gladys Laine seemed to be a ball of energy herself. I smiled at her, feeling a little wary but trying to mimic her cheerfulness.

"It was fine," I said. "Thanks for asking. I actually live on the west side, so I didn't have to drive through Philly."

"I've been to Philadelphia a handful of times, though all work related so I haven't seen much besides government buildings, but I'd love to go there just to see the sights some time." Gladys gave me another friendly smile as she ushered me over to a set of chairs with a small table tucked in between them.

"You'd like it, I'm sure," I said as I sat in the chair across from her, setting my purse down on the floor next to me.

"Ms. Laine, I…"

"Please, call me Gladys," she said, then reached out to pat my wrist. "I really am so sorry about Stella. She was a gem. I know everyone in Fox Cove is going to miss her."

"Thank you," I said. I watched her glance down at the phone in her hand as it dinged. She frowned as she looked at the screen. "Is everything alright?" I asked. "I could wait if you need to take care of that."

"What? Oh, no," she said shaking her head as she looked back up. "It's just my father. My mother is going in for a little surgery, very routine, but my father is such a worrier. He's been calling and texting me since five this morning. Honestly, these men. They'd fall right apart without us."

I smiled. "My dad is the same way."

Gladys patted my arm again. "Let's get you taken care of. I've got your aunt's files up in my office. We'll go up there to get them signed." She rose and went through the doorway. I followed here through and then up a narrow flight of stairs to the second floor. Gladys had turned the front bedroom into her office. The entry to the back bedroom had been widened and was open to the center room. The two rooms held bookcases filled with law books, a sitting area, and two sets of vertical wooden file cabinets.

I sat in the seat in front of her desk. She walked around to sit in her chair and reached for a stack of manila files and a large brown paperboard expanding envelope.

"I know your mom has already taken care of most of this with Stella. Stella was very organized that way. I guess she knew something like this might happen."

I didn't say anything. It was still new to me that Stella had had a heart condition. Gladys didn't seem aware of my silence as she shuffled through some papers. She pulled out a sheet and laid it down in front of me, turning it so I could read it.

"This is the basic release of Stella's estate. It says that I, as her executor, have met with at least one of her beneficiaries, or beneficiary's proxy, and am handing over all personal files, records, and miscellaneous items pertaining to the estate, including the house, contents, her blues, and one car. You and your mom are both named equally. I just need you to sign at the bottom."

I took the pen that she handed me and signed my name along the blank line, then handed the paper and pen back to her.

"And that's it," she said. "Now, I can answer any questions you might have, though I suggest you take the paperwork with you and go through it first. Oh, the keys are in the envelope." She held up the brown envelope.

"There's also a…" she looked over at her phone as it dinged again. She closed her eyes and sighed.

"It's OK," I said. "I understand. My dad really is the same way."

She smiled apologetically. "I'm sorry. I told him I'd be heading back today to be there with him."

"You're driving to Cleveland?" I asked.

"Yes, all packed and ready. I just wanted to get you settled first."

"Well, don't let me keep you." I reached for the files. "I'll do as you suggest and look through all of this, or at least get it to my mom for her to look through. If there's any questions, I'm sure she'll call you."

"Great!" She got up and waved me ahead of her. We went back down the stairs, and she held the front door open for me.

"It was so good to meet you, Deana. I hope we'll see more of each other. Take care."

"You too," I said as she waved and closed the door. I let out a breath and walked back to my car. I set the stack of files on the passenger seat, then reached for the envelope. Inside there was a smaller manila envelope and a ring of keys. I took out the keys, realizing they were for Stella's house. I grabbed the email printout from Gladys and read beneath the directions for the village. She had included another line with directions that must be for Stella's.

Turn left to go out towards valley, take 3rd right onto Winding Lane; road winds around the town, house is on the left, up the short gravel drive. If you reach Main St. You've gone too far!

CHAPTER FOUR

IT WAS A SHORT DRIVE to Stella's. The roads around the village seemed to circle around it, and as I drove up to the driveway to the house, I realized that I could see the ridge of the hill behind the village up ahead.

I turned in and drove along the gravel driveway, enjoying the trees that grew along the sides and touched overhead, creating a short, green, leafy tunnel. The house came into view, and I took a breath. It was beautiful.

It wasn't large. There was a door in the center, flanked by a window on either side. The second story repeated the first, with three windows lining up above the three openings below. It wasn't fancy, just a simple Georgian cottage that had been imported to colonial America along with settlers from England.

There was a green vine, probably ivy, trailing along part of the facade. The only other plants close to the house were a cluster of bushes on the right side. The drive expanded in front of the house so there was room to park two or three cars and still be able to back out without worrying about hitting anything.

I parked and grabbed the keys, my purse, and the files. It felt odd, walking into Aunt Stella's house, knowing she wasn't there anymore. I felt sad again, and a little guilty, for not making more effort to stay in touch.

There was a small entry hall in the center of the house, with a staircase leading to the second floor. What looked like a home office was immediately to my left. I went right and walked through a cozy living room that opened into a kitchen at the back. The ceiling above the living room was open to the rough wood rafters above, making the space appear large without losing the homey feeling. I passed by the overstuffed couch and into the kitchen area. Along the side wall of the kitchen was a large window. Through the glass I could see a beautiful garden.

I set my things down on the counter and continued walking through the kitchen to the back door. I opened it and was greeted with the sounds of multiple birds chirping. As I stepped out along the flagstone walkway, sweet herbal and floral smells drifted to me on the afternoon breeze. I took a deep breath, enjoying the calm feeling. I walked along the path, which led to a garden shed. It seemed large to me, but I didn't know a lot about maintaining a yard and garden so maybe it was a normal size for that. There was an odd, wire-enclosed structure on the side of the shed. It even had wire covering the top, like a large, human-sized bird cage.

Weird, I thought as I opened the shed to peek in. And then it got even stranger. Behind the door of the shed was a large space *not* filled with a lawn mower and gardening tools. Instead, the space contained about a dozen large hutches, and in them were extremely fluffy rabbits.

I must have stood at the shed door looking like a fool for I don't know how long, my eyes wide in disbelief and my mouth hanging open. Then a few of the rabbits moved a little and I jumped.

I shut the door to the shed softly, feeling like I needed to tiptoe away from them, not startle them. Can rabbits be startled?

I stumbled back into the house and shut the door. *This is insane*, I thought. I started to grab my stuff from the counter so I could walk back out of the house, lock the door, and call my mom to tell her to get her butt up here and deal with this. Then I set it all down again on the small table in the kitchen corner, took out the paperwork from the executor and read through it, slowly this time. When I got to the description of what the 'estate' of Stella Woods entailed I was even more confused.

"...personal files, records...house, contents, car...and the entity known as Star Woods Rabbitry, to include, but not limited to, the French angora blues. What in the hell is this?"

I grabbed my phone and scrolled down to Lilli's name. The phone barely rang before she picked up.

"Hey, De, how's your tri..."

"This is a mess!" I cut in. "The lawyer barely had time for me. I'm at a house full of rabbits. She left me blues, Lilli. Blues! I thought they'd be records or CDs...you know, music!"

"Um, De, calm down. You're not making any sense."

"They're rabbits, Lilli. Rabbits! My aunt Stella left me rabbits, and my mom too but she's not here. Who does that?"

"Deana, I need you to take a breath. Let's start from the beginning. Are you sitting down?"

I plopped into a chair at the kitchen table.

"I just can't believe this."

"De, start from the beginning. You met with the lawyer, right?"

"Yes, Gladys Laine. She's the executor for Aunt Stella's estate. I met her at her office. She had me sign some paperwork, started talking about the estate, but then she got a text and said something about her family in Cleveland, and she had to leave. She gave me the keys for Aunt Stella's house, and the legal files for the estate, and then…"

"And then? Deana, what happened?

I inhaled and shut my eyes, as if I could shut out the reality of the situation.

"De?"

"And then I drove here, to her house."

"OK, what's it look like, the house? Is it falling apart?"

"No, it's nice, I guess. Kind of simple, but not cheap or anything. It actually reminds me of the small homes in those Jane Austen movies."

"Well, that's not bad. You like Jane Austen."

I rolled my eyes. "Everyone likes Jane Austen, Lilli. And I know what you're doing."

"What?"

"You're trying to calm me down by making me talk about inconsequential details. You're doing your brain doctor thing."

Lilli laughed, "Yes, I am. Is it working?"

I blew out my breath and impatiently brushed hair out of my face. I still wasn't used to having shorter hair. "A little bit. Thanks, Lilli."

"It's what I do."

I smiled. Lilli had been working on her psychology degree when we met in grad school. Her twin sister, Rose, was getting her teaching degree. Lilli had worked at a few different places since then. For the past two years she had been working at a mental health clinic, focusing on people that lived or worked as primary caregivers in their families or jobs. A large percentage of her clients were stay-at-home or single parents, paid in-home caregivers or people that cared for disabled or elderly members of their family. She seemed to enjoy her work and I was happy for her, but I had a hard time being the one that was being analyzed, though I did appreciate her effort.

"Now I can imagine what the house looks like, and it sounds cute, so what happened next?"

"I walked through the kitchen, which you would love by the way. Aunt Stella may have liked simple things, but she has this fancy espresso maker that makes our coffee pot look like a clunky piece of junk."

"Ooh, that's my kind of lady."

"Yep, I think you two would have hit it off. I'm sorry I never got to introduce you." I felt the words catch in my throat and my eyes started to water. "It just always seemed like there would be time. I never felt like I had to push things, but now — now I feel like I need to try harder, to be more involved, more aware. And I'm really mad at my mom, which makes no sense."

"Oh, De, it's grief, and it's OK. Losing someone affects us all in different ways. Stella was important to you. Losing someone we know, especially when it's so unexpected, can be overwhelming. Just don't call your mom and yell at her. Whatever she did or didn't do, or didn't tell you, I'm sure she had a good reason for. I've met your mom. And as for Stella, you can tell me all about her when you're back in town. I'll have wine and chocolate waiting too."

I got up from the table and started walking through to the back door, like I had earlier. I continued explaining to Lilli.

"My mom is still going to hear from me about this, but I'll behave. Anyway, I walked outside and into the yard I saw through the kitchen window — it has flowers and herbs all over — and went back to the shed, just to peek in. I figured it would be full of yard tools, but it wasn't."

"What was in it?" Lilli asked.

"Like I said before, Lilli, rabbits. Cute, little, fluffy balls of bunny fur."

"Um..."

"Um? What does that mean? No brainy explanation, Lilli?"

"Well, De, this is actually a new one for me."

"How do you think I feel?" I whined. "What does this mean? Was Aunt Stella selling rabbits to magicians for their magic hat acts? Was she doing something illegal? Is it even allowed to have this many rabbits in one place?"

"That's a lot of questions. Ooh! I know. This is perfect for you, Deana."

"Excuse me? What part of this is perfect?"

"It's a mystery, a topic that you know nothing about. And what does my lovely librarian friend Deana Weber love to do?"

"Uh, Lilli, I don't think..."

"Research! Deana, you love to research. It's your *thing*."

"I do like to research," I said reluctantly.

"Great! So, this is what you'll do. You'll gather all the information you can about Stella, and her rabbits. You can go through her papers, books, call your mom — and remember to be nice — and figure out why Stella had rabbits."

"You make it sound so easy. This isn't just going through papers and files and reading books. There's real, live animals here. What am I supposed to do with them?"

"Hmm, good question. I better let you go so you can figure that out."

"Lilli!"

"Bye, De. I'll call to check in on you later. Just remember to breath and take things one step at a time."

"Bye, Doctor Hughes," I said sarcastically as I hung up.

LILLI WAS RIGHT, ONCE again. She was really annoying that way. I peeked through the window in the back door, eyeing the shed like it was full of snakes instead of fluffy bunny rabbits. Then I realized I was seeing a light shining through the small windows of the shed. *Were there lights on before?*

Suddenly I saw a shadow move inside of the shed. *That definitely wasn't there before.*

I jumped back from the window, trying to clear my head and slow my heart down. What should I do? Run? Call the police? Grab a knife?

No, I had to settle down. I took a deep breath, realized I had my cell in my hand still, and tiptoed back into the kitchen. I called 911, gave the dispatcher the address and told him that there was an intruder, maybe human or maybe a bear out in the shed behind the house. He told me to stay in the house and they would have an officer out to me. What did he think I was going to do, rush out to confront whoever it was? I'm not stupid.

But then I stopped pacing. What if it was a bear, and what if the bear was going to eat the rabbits? Do bears eat rabbits? I thought they only ate fish and plants, but I didn't really know. Is rabbit that different than fish to a hungry bear?

I looked around the kitchen. It wasn't that big. The old, round, wood pedestal table sat in the corner with three chairs around it. The counter was L-shaped with the espresso maker, a blender, and a toaster oven sitting on it, with some jars of spices and oils lined up beside the stove.

And then I remembered that bears don't like loud noises. I think a speaker at the library had spoken about it during a camping and hiking lecture. I looked around the kitchen again and then started opening the cabinets. I grabbed a shiny metal pot — that would be much louder than nonstick — and then dug through the drawers for a large utensil, finding a large metal spoon and a two-pronged meat fork. I chose the fork.

I moved back to the door that led out to the back yard, easing it open and stepping just outside of it. I didn't want to get too close. What if I succeeded in scaring it enough that it charged at me? I started hollering and clanging the fork against the pot. I didn't know how irritated the bear would get but my ear drums were certainly being abused.

Suddenly the door of the shed was yanked open. That's not a bear, I thought, just before a man stepped out. He was holding something in his hand. I jumped, shrieked, dropped my noise makers and ran back into the house, shutting the door and locking it. Then I ran to the front door and locked it, cowering down in front of it and praying that the police would get there before I was shot to death.

34

CHAPTER FIVE

AS I CROUCHED ON THE floor thinking of all of the horrible ways this could end, I heard a knock at the back door.

"Hello?" a deep voice called from outside the door.

I kept listening, getting more confused now than terrified, which I suppose is a step up as far as emotional responses can be judged.

"Hello, are you there?" the voice called again. "I'm going to come in, OK?"

Oh no he's not, I thought. *I locked the door.*

But then I heard a click and heard the door open and close. Why did the intruder have keys to the house?

I listened to the foot falls as the man walked through the kitchen, then watched as he came into view. He stopped just inside the entry to the kitchen.

"Um, Hi," he said as he gave a little wave.

I raised my hand and gave a very pathetic wave back but didn't say anything.

"I'm Garren Hewett. And you are?"

"Deana," I said, then realized how ridiculous I felt still crouched against the front door. I stood up slowly and said a little more confidently.

"I'm Deana Weber, and you're trespassing, Mr. Hewett."

He smiled. It was actually a nice smile. It reached his eyes and made small dimples appear in the pale brown skin of his cheeks.

He jangled the set of keys he held in his hand. "I've got keys, and permission from Stella to be here. I've been helping her with her rabbitry when I'm not working at the veterinary clinic. She paid me in advance, so I still have a few weeks left. Now, my question is — who are you? Ms. Laine said Stella's college friend would be coming to take care of her things, but *you* are not quite old enough to have gone to college with Stella."

"That's my mom," I said, "Aunt Stella's friend I mean, from college. She wasn't really my aunt, just...um," I realized I was jabbering and stopped talking, just standing there awkwardly.

"OK," Garren said. "I could show you some of what I've been doing. Do you know anything about rabbits? Is that a police car?"

He was looking out the window behind me. My mind registered that his broad shoulders stretched the material of his shirt very nicely when he moved, and then I turned and saw the flashing lights as the car pulled in. An officer stepped out, looked around, and then walked towards the house.

"Oh, crap," I uttered as I smacked my head. "I called the police." I looked back at Garren. "I'm sorry, but I saw something and thought it was a robber, or a bear, and I just, well...that's what you're supposed to do." I threw my hands up in exasperation. "You're supposed to call the police. I was being safe."

"Of course," Garren said, chuckling.

I was getting irritated with his amusement; I didn't care how cute his dimples were. I shook my head, deciding just to ignore him and opened the front door instead.

"Hi, Officer. I'm so sorry," Geesh, I was apologizing a lot. "I thought there was something, a bear or intruder, but it was just a friend of Stella's coming to take care of her rabbits."

The officer gave a curt nod. "No problem, ma'am. May I come in for a minute?"

"Oh, sure. Please, come in." I waved him in and shut the door.

"I'm Deana Weber. I called. Um, this," I said waving my hand towards Garren, "is Garren...uh."

"Hewett," the officer said. "Garren Hewett."

"Hey, Drew. How's it going?" Garren said as he nodded his head at the officer.

"Just fine. Pretty quiet until Ms. Weber called in."

"You two know each other?" I asked, looking back and forth at them.

"We're cousins," Garren said.

"On our mothers' side," Officer Drew finished. He turned to me and held out his hand. "Andrew Turner, but you can call me Drew," he said and smiled, his eyes twinkling at me.

I smiled back, feeling a little less sorry for making him come out.

"*Everyone* calls him Drew," Garren smirked.

"That's because everyone likes me," Drew shot back.

I was beginning to feel like there was a little bit of rivalry between these two guys.

"Well, I should probably take care of some things here before I get going," I said, trying to move things along.

"You're leaving?" They both asked.

"Yes, I just came in for the day to sign some paperwork. I live in Philly."

"Nice. I was just there for the Flyer's game. Do you like hockey?" Drew asked.

"Um, sure, I guess. I've gone to a couple of games with my roommate."

"Well, we'll have to meet up sometime when I'm in town."

"Oh, um, OK."

His radio went off and he turned away, pushed a button and spoke into it briefly. He turned back, smiled at me and said, "It was very nice meeting you, Deana. Call anytime if you need — anything." He winked at me, actually *winked* at me, then looked over at Garren and gave a quick nod as he opened the front door.

"Garren."

"Drew," Garren said.

Officer Turner walked back to his car, shutting his lights off as he pulled out of the driveway. I shut the door and turned back to Garren.

"Mr. Hewett, I really do have a lot to do before I leave."

"So, do you want me to show you the rabbitry or are you already familiar with it?"

"The what?" I asked.

"The rabbitry. The building out back, with the rabbits? It's called a rabbitry."

"Oh," I said." I didn't know that. Sure, yes, show me the rabbitry." I followed him through the kitchen, back out to the backyard, and into the shed, err, rabbitry.

We stepped inside. He ushered me in further so that he could close the door behind me. I was now shut in a building with a strange man I knew nothing about, except that he knew Aunt Stella. Though, when I thought about it, I also knew he was cousins with the cop. I relaxed a little and looked around the space.

"This is Stella's rabbitry. She called it Star Woods Rabbitry."

"What did she do with all of them?"

"There's not that many. And they're not as big as they look. Half of their size right now is all fur."

"I don't know why she left them to me and my mom. What are we supposed to do with all of these rabbits? I grew up in the suburbs. We had a dog. *One* dog. The closest I've been to farm animals was the 4-H show at the county fair." My voice was steadily rising, and I could feel my neck and face getting flushed.

"We have a 4-H club here. Lester Collins's sheep won a blue ribbon, went to the state fair and placed third," Garren said. He was standing next to me with his arms crossed in a relaxed pose.

"Are you humoring me?" I asked. "Do you think I'm going to flip out or something? I'm not flipping out." *Because I did that earlier before you got here*, I thought. "I'm fine. I just don't know what to do with — this." I held my arms out, encompassing the rabbits and everything else in the shed, or rabbitry as Garren called it.

"Right now, you don't have to do anything. I told you; Stella paid me in advance. I'll still come over to care for them."

"For a few weeks, sure, but then what?" I shook my head. "I need to call my mom. She's supposed to be here, not me. 'Just sign some papers,' she said."

"Well, they're fed for today. I'll be back in the morning to feed and groom them and let them out for some exercise."

"You do that every day? And you work at the veterinary clinic?"

Garren smiled. "No. I do have a life to live. I come over in the mornings and twice on Tuesday, Thursday, and Sunday. I'm off work from the clinic on Thursday and the weekend so Thursday and Sunday I spend some extra time here grooming the rabbits' coats and letting them out in the covered and fenced area outside here. As you can see from looking at them, these guys and gals have quite a bit of fur."

"Yeah, I noticed," I said as looked at the rabbits. "I've never seen rabbits that look like this. They look like huge gray cotton balls."

"They're angoras," Garren said laughing a little. "They've been bred for their wool for centuries, and they're a domesticated rabbit, so you wouldn't find them running around in the wild. They probably wouldn't survive. Most of these rabbits are blues. Stella always said their bluish gray coats calmed her."

I bit my lip, feeling tired and not very sure that I wanted to know anymore even though the academic part of me was curious. My exhaustion won out and I turned and walked back outside. Garren followed me, shutting the door and latching it.

"You said it's called a rabbitry?" I waved at the shed we were standing in.

"Yep, it just means a collection of rabbits."

"OK, well I need to make some calls and decide if I'm leaving or staying here tonight. Could you knock on the door in the morning just in case? I don't want to wake up and find a stranger in the kitchen. I know Stella knew you, and obviously trusted you, but it's just a little weird."

"No worries," Garren said, those cute dimples reappearing as he smiled at me. "I'll be here early anyway, and I don't usually go in the house. I'll probably be here and gone before you wake up."

"I get up pretty early. I'm used to an 8AM work schedule."

"Most farmers would consider that close to lunch time," Garren said. His smile grew wider, and I realized he was teasing me.

I sighed and held out my hand. "Well, if I don't see you, thank you — for taking care of the rabbitry, for helping Stella — and for not being a bear."

He laughed. "It was my pleasure. And maybe you or your mom can let me know what you decide about the rabbits? I can help find them good homes."

"I will, and thanks again. How did you get here anyway? I didn't see any other car out front."

"I don't live that far away. Sometimes I walk or bike over to get some exercise. My bike is out front."

"Oh, OK. Have a good ride home."

After Garren left I locked the house up and dug around in Stella's fridge for something to eat. I found some pickles, basic condiments, quite a few Hershey's chocolate bars, some stone ground wheat bread, and cheddar cheese slices. I went for a full meal of carbs: cheese and mayo sandwich with a Hershey bar on the side. I took my plate and a glass of water and sat at the pedestal table in the kitchen.

The table sat next to the large window that looked out over the garden between the house and rabbitry. The sun had already moved across the sky in the late afternoon, dappling the garden with shadows from the buildings and trees around it. Half the sandwich disappeared as I stared out at the idyllic scene. I turned back towards the room and saw the files were still stacked on the table where I had left them earlier.

I pulled the top one off and opened it as I ate. It held banking information, paperwork for a car, and some life insurance forms. I closed it and set it aside, reaching for the next file. This one was thicker and labeled Star Woods Rabbitry. I flipped it open and found sheets with charts that looked like genealogies. The tops of the sheets were titled, Rabbit Pedigree, with lines off to the side filled in with information about the rabbitry, owner, and contact. I glanced at the charts briefly and shut the folder. I'd had enough with rabbits for one day.

I took the chocolate and got up, walking into the living room. Stella had a small TV on a shelf of the entertainment center, but most of the space was set up to play music. A few shelves were filled with CDs, while more shelves held collections of vinyl records. There was a very impressive CD player, a record player, and a large black box whose wires led to multiple speakers placed around the room.

I pulled one of the records out and looked at the cover. It was a recording of songs by Billie Holiday. I vaguely recognized the name. I think I had watched a movie about her starring Diana Ross. I looked at a few more titles. Stella had a large collection of blues music. I only recognized a few of the names, like Stevie Ray Vaughan and Charlie Patton. Others, like Memphis Minnie and Big Mama Thornton, I had never heard of. Another section had music by Frank Sinatra and a lot of show tunes. There were also sections of soft rock and folk rock, like Stevie Nicks and Fleetwood Mac, Carly Simon, Bonnie Raitt, Janis Joplin, Tina Turner, and Joni Mitchell.

"Blues music and blue rabbits. Who were you, Aunt Stella?" I looked at the last record sleeve I had pulled out. The singer, B.B. King, was pictured on the front, a cigarette in his mouth and the smoke curling up and around him. I slid the record back into the stack.

This really wasn't the way to research something; hunting around with no clear idea of what I was looking for. I knew what I had to do. I finished the chocolate and picked up my phone from where I had set it on the edge of the couch. I scrolled through and pressed the call option for my parents. It was late enough in the day that my mom might be home from work. She answered with a cheerful hello.

"Hello, Mom," I said with fake cheer.

"Hi sweetheart. Did you get to Fox Cove okay? How did the meeting go with the executor? Ms. Laine seemed very nice when I spoke with her."

"Oh, she was, and yes, I got here just fine. I'm still here actually."

"Really? But it's so late, Deana. Should you be driving back to Philadelphia at this time? You're bound to get stuck in rush hour traffic, and after you've already been driving a few hours; that concerns me."

"Really?" I said, imitating her. "You know what concerns me, Mom? How about the fact that Aunt Stella has a shed full of rabbits. Did you know about that, Mom?"

"Of course I did, Deana. I saw them when I went to visit Stella last year. I'm sure I told you about them. Aren't they cute, like big balls of silky cotton."

"No, Mom. You did *not* tell me. I think I would have remembered."

"I'm sure I did."

I closed my eyes and prayed for patience. I had told Lilli I wouldn't yell. Though, beating my head on a wall right now sounded like a very good idea.

"Mom, when are you coming up here so all of this stuff can be taken care of? I signed for all of the files and have them with me. Do you want me to mail them to you?"

"I'm not sure," she said distractedly. "There's so much going on with this waterfront expansion. Did I tell you about that? The city planning office is so busy. I'm attending a meeting Thursday, and the EPA will be there. Then next week we have meetings almost every day. A lot of groups and businesses are concerned about the impact to the river and the Intracoastal Waterway."

God help me and give me patience, I thought as I gritted my teeth. "Sounds interesting, Mom, but there's an entire house of stuff here to go through, and rabbits. Did I mention the rabbits?"

"Oh, Deana. Don't worry. Isn't that nice, young man there? Stella had him helping her with things. He's a veterinary technician, did you know? What was his name, Garret, Gavin?"

"Garren. His name is Garren, and he's still here. But I don't know how much longer he'll be helping. Do you plan on paying him for his time?"

"Stella took care of that for a while, I'm sure of that. Maybe you could hold on to the files for now. I can get them from you later."

I was suddenly feeling tired.

"I think I'm just going to sleep here tonight and drive back to Philly tomorrow."

"Will your boss be okay with that? I don't want you to get in trouble at work. Weren't you telling me last month that you were going to try for a management position? You'll have to work extra hard to be considered, Deana. You know that. I've told you often enough; women always have to work harder to get half as far as men."

"I know, Mom, but it's not really an issue anymore." I took a deep breath and then spit it out before I changed my mind. "I was laid off."

"Oh, Deana," my mom sighed. Her end of the line got quiet, uncharacteristically so.

"Are you still there?" I asked.

"Yes, just thinking of what you should do next."

That was the mom I knew and loved and who drove me a little crazy, always planning the next step.

"I'm figuring it out, Mom. Don't worry."

"I'm your mother, Deana. I always worry, but I also know you're going to be fine."

"Thanks, Mom."

"I love you, Deana."

"Love you too."

We ended the call after I assured her again that I would figure out what I was doing next. I texted Lilli to let her know I'd be back tomorrow. She replied with a smiley face and wine glass emoji. It's always comforting to know there are people in the world who understand you.

Since I had decided to spend the night, I looked around for some sheets to cover the couch with. There was a quilt rack along one wall. I took one off and spread it on the couch. Once that was done, I was at a loss of what to do. I still had a few hours before I could even think of going to sleep. I went back over to the stereo and played around with the buttons and dials until I had figured out how to turn on the turntable. I chose one of the records and in a few seconds Stevie Nicks was singing 'Landslide' through the surround sound speakers that Stella had set up around the room. I hummed along as I walked around the house.

I imagined Stella in this house, listening to her music, reading the books she had on shelves in her study. I browsed through the books. There were many about travel and foreign countries. I remembered all of the postcards my brothers and I used to get from Stella. Pictures of far-off countries stamped with colorful stamps in foreign languages. I smiled as I thought of how I always wanted her to take me with her. Sadly, I was one of those less-traveled Americans. I had one solitary stamp in my passport book, from a school trip to Canada.

I looked through the rest of Stella's books. She had some modern and classic fiction, mysteries, quite a few on rabbits, and some history and biographies. I definitely didn't have a shortage of reading material. I took a leather-bound copy of

Sherlock Holmes stories with me as I continued my exploration.

The next room down the hall and beside the study looked like the master bedroom. Stella's room. I didn't go in. Instead, I shut the door and walked upstairs, glancing in the two rooms up there. One was set up as a guest room but had bins stacked around it. The other room looked like it was being used for more storage. The space over the living room that would have also been a bedroom had been exposed up to the ceiling, so I could look down into the living room. I walked back downstairs just as the record ended.

I settled into the quilt covered couch with the book and started reading about foggy moors and supernatural hounds.

CHAPTER SIX

FILTERED SUNLIGHT WOKE me up the next morning and I opened my eyes, feeling disoriented until I remembered where I was. My phone display let me know that I had slept past eight. I stood up and stretched, feeling better than I thought I would after sleeping on a couch. I rehung the quilt and then went to the bathroom, washed my face and looked in the mirror to check how mussed my hair was. Soap and water and a quick comb through my hair made me look presentable enough. I didn't have a toothbrush, so I just swished some mouthwash and spit it out. It was enough to wake me up so I could drive back to Philadelphia where I would happily take a shower and wait for Lilli to get home so we could open a bottle of wine and I could fill her in on this mess. If nothing else positive came from this trip, Rose would be happy to know that I had had that adventure she was hoping for.

I grabbed my purse and the stack of files. As I was walking from the living room to the front foyer, I looked over to Stella's study again. On a whim I went over to the bookshelves and took a couple of books that I had noticed last night, then locked the door and hopped in my car, glancing towards the garden and rabbitry on my way out. I hadn't seen Garren but assumed he had already come to feed the bunnies. I was glad he was still caring for them, even if it wasn't for much longer. I hoped my mom had some kind of plan.

I took a left out of Stella's driveway in the hopes that the road would lead back into town. If not, I'd have to turn around and head back the way I had come yesterday. I was rewarded when I got to a hard curve in the road and saw the street sign change from Winding Lane to Main Street. The first business I passed was a cafe called the Sparrow. It was built in what looked like a remodeled farmhouse. The exterior was pale blue with white trim. The second story windows had window boxes full of small spring flowers. A few chairs and tables were set outside on the covered porch. I parked along the street and walked up the short sidewalk to the front door. I could smell brewing coffee as soon as I opened it and took a deep breath, feeling some of the tension from yesterday leave my body.

Most of the tables inside were taken. The cafe seemed popular, even at nine on a Tuesday morning. I got in line and continued to look around. There were multiple mobiles hanging from the ceiling. On each mobile wires branched out from a center post hanging from the ceiling. Some of the wires were straight and plain metal, some twisted. They ended in what looked like paper mâché figures: most of them different versions of what I assumed were sparrows, some butterflies or dragonflies, some fanciful shapes. I had a moment of understanding why babies stared in fascination at the mobiles placed over their cribs. It was hard to look away from the slowly rotating objects.

"Hi, are you ready to order? Mam?"

I looked at the woman behind the counter, slowly coming out of my mobile-induced daze. "Huh? Oh, yes, sorry."

She laughed and said, "That's OK. We get a lot of that reaction from first timers."

"They're beautiful."

"They're made locally. Do you know what you want?" she asked, trying to take my order again.

"Yes, thanks, a medium latte. Actually, I'll try that saspa-nilla latte, and an egg and cheese croissant, to-go please."

"Good choice. It's a seasonal flavor, so let us know how you like it."

"I'm actually leaving today, but I'm sure it's good."

I paid and stepped towards the end of the counter where a few other people were waiting for their orders. One woman looked over at me as she was talking to the barista at the espresso station. She smiled and moved towards me.

"Well, you're a new face. Moving in or just passing through?"

"Oh, I'm just passing through," I said. "My aunt lives here, I mean she did live here. She passed away recently."

The woman's hand flew to her chest, and she said breathlessly, "You don't mean Stella Woods? Are you Deana? Oh my God, you *are* Deana. Why, Stella showed pictures of you and your brothers to us all of the time. She was so proud of all of you." She held her hand out and I took it to shake, but she covered it with her other hand.

"I'm Gwendolyn Fauks. I own Foxie Fibers; the yarn and craft shop next door. I go by Gwen, though. It's so nice to meet you, Deana. Trini, did you know this is Stella's niece?" Gwen said to a woman passing by us. She took the woman's arm to stop her. "We're all so sorry about Stella. She's going to be missed in this village." Gwen said. "Isn't that right, Trini?"

The woman gave Gwen a suffering look, then looked over at me. Her features softened a little and she said, "Stella was a good duck. My condolences." Then she resumed her walk, disappearing behind a door marked 'employees only'.

"Trini owns the Sparrow. Her name's really Trinity. Trinity Loughlin. I think I heard that she used to be a nun. Anyway, we were all so shocked by Stella's passing."

I felt like I was having the conversation again with Gladys Laine. I still wasn't sure how to react, so I didn't say anything, just gave a small nod.

"We had a small service at the church for her. It wasn't her thing as I'm sure you know, but it helped the village. I don't think she would have minded. She did have spiritual feelings."

"It sounds nice. I'm sure she would have liked it."

Gwen beamed at me. "Well, you come back and visit any time."

I thanked Gwen Fauks and when my order was ready, I took it and left, giving Gwen a little wave.

I was in such a rush to leave the cafe and the well-meaning woman that I didn't pay a lot of attention to what was around me until a voice called my name. I looked over and saw Officer Turner.

"Heading out," he called. He was standing near a newspaper dispenser in front of the cafe.

"Yep, back to the city," I called back, continuing to walk in the direction of my car.

"Drive carefully, and don't worry about those rabbits. Garren will keep the bears away."

I gave him a fake smile as I stepped off of the curb. He laughed. There was an older man sitting on the bench next to the dispenser. He looked at both of us and shook the paper he was reading loudly, as if we were interrupting his privacy by talking on a public sidewalk.

"Good morning, Mr. Martin," Drew said to the grumpy man as he tipped his hat and walked towards the cafe with his paper.

I had to squeeze sideways to get in my car and almost spilled my coffee. I looked at the car next to me. It was shiny and bright blue. The seats inside looked expensive. They were probably leather. As I pulled out, I looked over at it, noticing the Tesla emblem on the back. There was a bright green sticker on the rear window that had a marijuana leaf circled by a rainbow. If I had the money to buy that car, I would think about learning how to park it better. I could have easily banged my door into it and not felt the least bit sorry about leaving a scratch. *Idiots with bank accounts*, I thought. *You can find them everywhere.*

CHAPTER SEVEN

THE NEXT MORNING LILLI poked her head in my bedroom before she left for work, made enough noise to be sure I was awake and then disappeared. I threw the covers off and stood up and stretched, feeling surprisingly good. Why was I surprised? I had done a favor for my mom, had admitted to her that I was jobless, and I was now back home and ready to job hunt in earnest.

I walked out to the kitchen and made my coffee, taking it with me to the couch where I had left my laptop the night before. It's a small apartment. Lilli and I try to keep it organized by not leaving papers, tech accessories, or anything else laying around, but she had understood last night when she left me in this same spot around eleven. I had cleaned up a little by stacking files and papers on top of my closed laptop on the small coffee table when I finally went to bed. I knew she had been OK with the small mess because she had left one of her fancy energy bars on top of my pile, probably her way of telling me to keep going and not wallow. It was a bad habit I had. Wallowing, or procrastinating. Whatever you wanted to call it.

I was doing good though. I had a fresh, updated resume, a small list of possible job leads, and even a few responses from the networking messages I had sent out through LinkedIn. I drank my coffee as I read through them, noting a couple that looked promising. My eyes strayed to the stack of books and files I had brought back from Fox Cove, and I frowned. I got up and grabbed one of the books. It looked old, with a faded blue cover. The title was *Completely Angora*, with the drawing of a rabbit in the center and what looked like Celtic style scrolling around the edges. I looked closer and noticed more rabbits drawn into the scrolling. It was pretty, though a little odd. I flipped it open.

"Wow, this is extensive," I said to myself as I looked at the Table of Contents. It listed what looked like over fifty topics: from Why Angora?, Nest Box, and Culling, to Urine Burn, Scatology — whatever that was — , and Weaving Angora. I flipped through the pages, reading paragraphs here and there, and looking at the photos. I couldn't believe all of the work that went into taking care of one little animal.

I set the book aside and picked up another one that I had brought back. This one was a book on the history of blues music. I knew Stella was from Chicago originally. She was always pushing us to cheer for the Chicago Cubs, and I knew, distantly, that Chicago had a connection to blues music. I had had the thought while I was looking through her music that it was odd to me that Stella had such a large blues and rock collection; then I mentally slapped myself. Why would that be odd? Why did I think it was normal for her to have show tunes and Sinatra but not Billie Holiday and Fleetwood Mac? I was making assumptions about a fifty-year-old woman that I only knew through the eyes of a little girl and then as a teenager. For all I knew Stella could have been a roadie with AC/DC.

My coffee was gone, and I knew I had to get myself off of the couch and out of the apartment. After grabbing something to eat and getting dressed I decided to drive to my old job and then grab some things to make dinner. First though I gathered the dirty clothes and started a load of laundry.

Later in the day, I pulled into the library parking lot, parking in one of the thirty-minute slots. I figured if I felt too awkward it would give me an excuse to rush back out.

Matilda, a junior library aide, rushed over when she saw me walk in. "Deana, I'm so glad to see you! Are you coming back?"

"No, just here to look up some things." Her face fell. She was still finishing her degree and hadn't quite lost her shiny, idealistic ignorance. I hoped she was able to hold on to it for longer than I had.

"It's OK, Matilda. I've already been working on something new." It was true, technically, and vague enough that she made the assumption that I meant a new library position. I watched her perk up again and felt a little envious of her naivete. I promised her I'd come back in to visit and headed off to the computers to look through the catalog. In no time I had found some books on fiber farms and had checked out a couple to take home. I saw my old boss, George Lewis, through the large window that looked into his office. He waved briefly at me and then went back to talking with the people sitting across from him. I checked out my books at the automated checkout stand and then left, still feeling a little awkward, but also better. I had liked working for the library co-op and wanted to leave that bridge intact in case there was a future opportunity to come back.

Dinner ended up being a frozen, but organic, casserole. It was pre-made from the specialty foods market Lilli liked to shop at, and the pasta in it was some kind of rice so I felt that she would approve, even if it wasn't made from scratch. I turned the oven on to preheat as I read the directions. It was already after four and the casserole would take almost an hour to cook, so it would be ready right around the time Lilli got home. I felt almost domestic as I moved the clothes from the washer to the dryer, then started a second load of towels washing.

As I began picking up the stuff that I had left on the coffee table and moving it into my room, my cell phone rang. It showed a Pennsylvania number but not one I knew.

"Hello?" I answered.

"Deana? This is Garren Hewett, from Fox Cove."

"Um, hi. How did you get my number?"

"Ms. Laine, the executor gave it to me. I called her first, but she felt under the circumstances I should speak with you."

"Under what circumstances?" I asked.

"One of the rabbits has been stolen — I think."

"You think? What does that mean?"

"Mudd, that's the rabbit that's missing, he's had a tendency to escape from time to time. He's quick and, like most rabbits, likes to dig."

"OK, so maybe he just got loose. Why do you think he was stolen?"

"These hutches are very well secured. Mudd was her first rabbit and Stella learned most of his tricks, so she took extra precautions with the hutches, rabbitry building and their play area. Even if they dig outside there's a few inches of the fencing buried so they can't dig right under it. And the hutch, it wasn't latched, but it was closed. If he had gotten it open somehow, I would think that it would still be cracked open."

"So, what does this mean?" I stood in my room frowning once again. I was doing that a lot. At my age it wasn't a good habit. I rubbed my forehead, trying to erase the tension I felt building up.

"I think it means that someone stole him. I think you or your mom should call the police, or I can do it from here. I just thought it should be your decision."

As if I wanted *that* responsibility. I sighed. I really did want him to handle it but knew that wasn't fair of me. And I still wasn't convinced this was really a crime. It was a country village, for Pete's sake. Who would go around stealing rabbits?

I chewed on my lip, already regretting what I was about to say.

"I think I should come out there. I could be there around seven. I just need to wait for my roommate to get home. Then I'll decide from there whether to involve the police or not. Would you be able to meet me at the house or do you have plans?"

"It's Wednesday so there's karaoke at the pub, but I suppose I can skip my solo this week." He gave a quick laugh. "That was a joke."

I rolled my eyes and smiled. "Thanks, Garren. I appreciate it. I'll see you soon."

I hung up, then tossed my cell on the bed and plopped down next it. I just wanted to crawl under the covers and close my eyes.

Damn Rose Evans and her hopes for country adventures.

"Suck it up, De," I said to myself as stood back up. I grabbed my overnight bag from under my bed and started pulling together a few changes of clothes. Hopefully I could drive back to Fox Cove, find out Mudd the missing rabbit was the escape artist he had a reputation of being, and we would find him munching wildflowers in a field somewhere. Then I could sleep on Stella's couch again and drive back here tomorrow and get on with my life, however questionable it might be at the moment.

CHAPTER EIGHT

STILL WANTING TO MAKE dinner for Lilli, I put the casserole in the preheated oven, then went into the bathroom and put together some toiletries, adding them to my bag. The dryer buzzed and I took out the clothes, dumping them on the couch and going back to move the towels from the washer to the dryer. I was just finishing my folding when I heard Lilli's key in the door.

"Well, well," she said as she came in and saw me, "it looks like someone's been a busy bee today. And what's that smell? Did you cook?" She put her stuff onto the coffee table next to the clothes, picked up a pile that she knew was hers and started to carry it to her room.

"Ha," I said, knowing she was teasing me. She was very aware that me and the oven were not on good terms. "I picked up one of those healthy and fancy meals you like so much. It should be ready any minute." I stood up and grabbed one of the piles of clothes. "And I hope you enjoy it because I now have to drive back to Fox Cove." I left the pile on my bed and walked back to the kitchen.

"Again? Why?" she asked as she came into the kitchen.

"There's a missing rabbit. Can you believe that? A rabbit—missing, and I have to drive there to look for it before admitting that it's been stolen and calling the police."

"You think it was stolen?"

I don't know," I said with exasperation. "Garren Hewett — the guy I told you about who's taking care of them — called and said he thinks it was stolen. But there's also a chance that the rabbit just got out and ran off, because he's done that before."

Lilli started laughing, then saw my face and pursed her lips, trying to stop. Then she started again.

"I'm sorry," she said as she gave me a hug. "It's just so…hilarious. I mean, you, Deana Weber, running all over the state, chasing an escaped rabbit. It's like a cartoon."

"Yes, it's so funny," I said dryly. "Next thing you know, a piano will drop on my head."

I finished getting my travel bag together and set it by the front door.

I walked back into the kitchen again.

"Pull the casserole out when the oven timer goes off. Then let it cool for five to ten minutes before you cut into it."

"Do you want any help with your stuff?" Lilli asked as she opened the fridge and pulled out a bottle of wine.

"No, I've got it. I'm just taking an overnight bag and some reading material."

"Oh, and don't forget you phone charger," she said.

"Thanks, I forgot that."

I went back in my room, grabbed my charger and stuffed it in my purse. I put all the files and books in a canvas bag. It had an Outerbanks, NC logo on it. I had picked it up last year on one of my trips to see my family. Thinking of my family reminded me that I would need to call my mom at some point. I decided to wait until I was sure about the rabbit being stolen or running off. There was no reason to make her worried before I knew exactly what had happened.

I was back on the road less than thirty minutes after Lilli got home. If I didn't hit too much rush hour traffic then I should be back in Fox Cove only a little later than seven, which is the time I had told Garren.

While I was still an hour away from the village, Garren texted me that he would be a little late. My cell phone automatically connects to my car audio with its Bluetooth option so I listened to his text and then used voice response to answer him so I wouldn't have to pull over to text him back.

After a much quicker and more stressful drive back to the village I pulled up in front of Stella's house and parked. It was so quiet, I almost felt like I was in a horror film and waiting for the monster to jump out of the bushes. I shook my head at my overactive imagination. I had been living in the city so long I had forgotten what a quiet country evening sounded like.

I grabbed the few bags I had brought and went inside, dumping everything on the floor by the couch.

As I walked through the kitchen to the back door I flipped on lights, brightening the interior of the house against the fading sunset. It took a couple tries of the multiple switches on the wall next to the door but I finally found the outside flood lights and turned them on, then walked out into the yard. There were insects buzzing around some of the flowers, some bumblebees, smaller bees and bugs, and a few birds darted around, their chirping breaking into the silence of the evening.

I opened the door to the rabbitry, knocking lightly in case Garren was already inside.

Some of the rabbits moved in their hutches as I stepped inside. I could hear their scuffling though I couldn't see them very well in the waning light. I felt along the wall and found a switch box that had been attached to the frame. The space became lit with a soft pinkish light, and I could see more of the rabbits moving around, probably thinking I had come in to feed them.

"Sorry guys," I said quietly. "I don't have any goodies for you."

There were six along the right side, three up at eye level, and three below them, almost even with my hips. That left a few feet of space open above the floor. The left side was set up the same way, but with three hutches up and only two down. The last two hutches were along the back wall, again one above the other. Under each hutch was a solid tray that looked like it could be pulled out. To the right of the rear hutches were shelves with bins and what I assumed were supplies for the rabbits.

There was a short barrier about three feet in from the doorway. I stepped over it and moved along the rows of hutches. The floor was covered with multi-colored rubber mats that interlocked with each other like a puzzle. Stella had formed a simple rug design with the mats that made the space feel cozy.

The first upper hutch had a pale gray rabbit in it whose fur floated around its body. The fur had to be over three or four inches long and I couldn't resist reaching out to touch it. The rabbit was close enough that my fingers barely had to go through the hutch wires before I felt the soft, fluffy texture. The rabbit moved a little but didn't attempt to get away, so I began to lightly pet its fur. I looked at the tag that was fixed to the tray at the bottom of the hutch.

"Bessie. Well, hello, Bessie. You're a pretty girl," I cooed. "If I'm bothering you just hop away, but please don't bite me. Do you bite?"

Bessie the rabbit continued to nibble on some straw, ignoring me completely. I withdrew my fingers and looked over at the hutch next to her.

"Fleetsie," I read off of that tag, then looked at the hutches below and beside them, making my way towards the back as I went.

"Rainey, Ella Bella, Joplin, Billie Bee."

I moved over to the back hutches. The top one read Howler. The rabbit inside was a deep black with shots of white. I looked at the tag for the hutch below. It read Muddy Waters. The hutch was empty. So, this was the escaped or stolen rabbit, Mudd.

I looked at the name again, then looked back at the other tags I had read.

"She named you after her blues, jazz, and rock singers," I said out loud. The rabbits didn't seem very impressed with my deduction, just continued chewing their straw and licking their fur. "Well, I'm impressed with myself," I said airily as I walked down the left side, reading the tags as I went. This side had a mix of male and female names on the tags: two males named Vaughan and HRH BB, and three more females named Shemi, Ruthie, and Popi V. I didn't recognize their names but was sure that if I looked back through Stella's music that I would find singers that matched these rabbits as well.

I walked back to Muddy Water's hutch. The door was unlatched like Garren had said it was. I reached down and opened it, noticing how it didn't automatically swing shut. Garren had been right; if the rabbit had gotten out on its own the door would still have been ajar.

I walked back into the house just in time to see a pair of headlights curve along the walls and reflect through the front windows. Garren was shutting the door to his truck as I opened the front door. He had a large paper bag in his hand and as he walked towards me, I smelled something delicious coming from whatever was in it.

My stomach rumbled loudly just as I stepped aside to let him in.

"Sorry," I said, "I didn't realize how hungry I was until I smelled whatever you have in there." I gestured towards the bag.

"No worries. I figured you might not have eaten. This," he said, holding up the bag, "is why I was running late. I stopped and picked up food for us. I hope you like lamb stew and camembert."

"That sounds amazing, but let me pay you for part of it, please."

"No," he said, fully dismissing my offer. He broke into a grin and chuckled. "My parents own the restaurant, The Drake. I get a very good family discount; all I can eat if I wash a few dishes."

"Well, thank you then, and thank you for coming back here tonight. Let me get some plates and utensils and we can eat while we try to figure this out."

I walked ahead of him into the kitchen.

"I'm not sure there's much besides water to drink. I didn't see a lot in the fridge the last time I was here. God, that was just two days ago."

"Water is fine."

We sat at the pedestal table in the kitchen, and I tried very hard not to inhale everything that Garren had brought. We started with a loaf of artisan bread. Garren sliced it and spread a couple of pieces with the softened Camembert cheese. He handed me one of the slices and I bit into it, chewed and tasted the creamy tartness of the cheese mixing with the crusty earthiness of the bread.

"Mmm, this is so good." I was almost finished with the cheese and bread when he set one of the warm bowls of stew in front of me.

"Here, this will be even better."

The warm air from the stew curled up and I inhaled the rich smell before dipping my fork in. I speared some lamb and vegetables and brought it to my mouth, feeling the rich-flavored broth drip onto my tongue right before I took the bite. I chewed and swallowed and immediately took another bite. Then I reached for another slice of bread he had set out on a plate.

"This is amazing," I mumbled as I chewed the delicious slice of baked bread slathered with an herb butter that he had also brought. There were three more little plastic containers of it and I was hoping that he would be leaving any leftovers from the meal with me.

"I'll tell my parents you enjoyed it. My dad bakes most of the bread. He learned when he was growing up. His mother, my *grandmere*, taught him."

"*Grandmere*? So, you're French?"

"Technically, yes. Though if you ask my dad, he'll say he's Norman."

"So, your family's from Normandy? If all the food there is like this, I might have to move." I dunked a small corner of my bread in the stew and ate it, making more humming noises.

Garren laughed. "Yes, I can see that you're enjoying it."

"Sorry," I said as I dabbed a napkin at my mouth.

"Make all the noise you want. I believe in some countries it's polite to burp after a meal if you've enjoyed it."

"Um, I don't think I'll be doing that." I smiled, then reached for my glass of water. I took a drink and then took a deep breath. I really wanted to eat more but I was feeling very full. I reluctantly pushed my bowl of stew away from me. "I think I'm done. That was so good. Thank you."

Garren wiped the last of his stew from his bowl with a slice of bread. "Let me help you clean up," he said as he started to rise.

"Nope, you brought dinner. I'll clean up. Do you want to take any of this with you."

"No, you can keep it. I can get more anytime."

I smiled. "I was hoping you'd say that." I found some plastic storage containers and put what was left of my stew in one, the cheese in another, and the bread in a plastic bag, then put it all plus the butter containers in the fridge.

Garren had walked out to the living room and was looking through Stella's music collection when I came in. He chose a CD case. He turned on the system, put a CD in and pushed a button, skipping over some songs. He adjusted the volume and some of the knobs. The room was suddenly full of background instruments and the drawn-out notes on an electric guitar. Then a rough, deep voice started singing. I felt chills along my shoulders and closed my eyes.

"You like it?" Garren asked.

"I do, yes. Who is it?"

"Howlin' Wolf. My dad saw him sing this in London in the 60s. It's called 'Spoonful'. I never got why he liked the music so much. He didn't really explain it to me. Then I met Stella. She had brought in a baby rabbit to the clinic. I mentioned that Howler was an odd name for a cute little rabbit as I was checking them in. And I got a history lesson on Chester Burnett, aka, Howlin' Wolf." He smiled as he looked at the CD case.

"She invited me over after that, and we would listen to blues and jazz music, even some of the rock ladies she liked, while she talked about growing up in Chicago or the places she had traveled to. Sometimes she would groom a rabbit as she talked or pluck its wool depending on the time of year. Their fur grows full every three or four months, and then they need to have it removed."

"Why? Isn't it like other animals, helps cool them and keep them warm?"

"Angoras are a domestic breed. They've been bred to have the coats they do, but even if they start molting — shedding their coats — they may get a lot of matted fur which could cause skin issues. Also, rabbits groom themselves like cats. They're very clean that way, but unlike a cat they can't throw up hairballs. If they ingest too much of their fur it can cause GI problems."

"GI problems?"

"They get constipated," he said very seriously.

"Oh, well, yeah, that would suck," I said. He grinned and I laughed a little, breaking the awkwardness of the topic.

Garren turned the volume down a little and went to sit down.

"Look, I think we should call the police. I don't think Mudd just got out."

"I know," I sighed as I folded myself onto the couch. I tucked my knees up but kept my shoes on the edge. "I went out there after I got here. I looked at the door of Mudd's hutch. You're right, he didn't just get out. Someone must have taken him."

"I know it's late. If you don't want people out here tonight, I could call Drew, my cousin. You met him the other day when you thought I was a bear."

I grimaced. "Officer Turner, I remember." I thought about it.

"Yes, call him. Tell him what you found. I'll talk to him too and plan to meet him in the morning."

"I brought a lock also so you can secure the rabbitry, if you want. I don't think whoever took Mudd will be back. It would have been easier to take the rabbits all at once if they had wanted to take them all but locking it up might make you feel better."

"Sure. That sounds like a good idea."

We made the call to Drew Turner. He said he'd start a report on the scene as Garren described it, but he wanted us both to see him in person. Garren agreed to meet him later the next day. I told him I could meet him at the house in the morning. He was fine with that. Garren went out to the rabbitry and locked it up, handing me one of the keys and putting the other on his key ring. I said goodbye to him after I assured him repeatedly that I would be fine at the house by myself. I locked the door once I finally got him to leave, then decided to leave on the outside lights, just in case.

CHAPTER NINE

I SLEPT FITFULLY AND woke up hours before sunrise. I laid on the couch dozing until I heard a car pull in. I got up and looked out the window, saw Garren step out of his truck and go through the side gate into the yard. I debated getting dressed and going out to help, but then decided I'd rather just lay down a little longer. When I heard him leave a little later, it was starting to lighten up outside. I got back up and turned off the outside lights, then went to the bathroom. When I came back out, I walked into the kitchen and looked at Stella's fancy espresso machine. Coffee did sound good, but I decided I wasn't up for figuring out the shiny appliance this morning. Instead, I showered, got dressed, and then waited for Officer Andrew Turner to arrive.

At 9 AM on the dot I saw Officer Turner's patrol car pull in front of the house. I was walking around outside in the garden, trying to test my very limited knowledge of plants and herbs. So far, I had been able to identify yarrow, rosemary, and what I thought was parsley, but may also be basil. There was also a large space filled with lavender bushes towards the back of the house. Next to the door to the kitchen there was a small greenhouse that I had walked by on my first trip here. I was just about to peek inside when I heard the car.

I looked towards the front of the house and saw the patrol car pulling in. I went back inside and washed my hands before walking through the house to meet him at the front door. That's when I noticed the time on the microwave and hoped this would be quick so I could run into the village for coffee and breakfast. He was just about to knock when I opened the door.

"Well, good morning," he said, quickly hiding his surprise behind a bright smile.

"Good morning, Officer. Come in, please."

He stepped inside and I shut the door, walking towards the couch to sit. He sat down in a chair near me and pulled out a pad and pen. For a moment, though, he just sat there and looked at me. Then he said, very seriously, "Are you OK, Ms. Weber? I know a theft can be a very emotional experience."

"I'm alright. I think I'm more confused than upset at the moment. It just seems like such an odd thing to steal."

"Obviously the thief thought there was some value in the rabbit; whether that value is monetary or personal is what's going to help us track them down. Do you know very much about Stella's, I mean Ms. Woods's rabbits? Where they're from, what they're worth, who else knew that she kept them?"

I shook my head, feeling useless. "I don't know anything about them. Garren can probably help you the most with those questions. I was only here before to sign paperwork. My mom and I are both beneficiaries, but she's been the one dealing with Aunt Stella's estate."

"I see." He wrote some things down in his book.

"Do you know if the rabbit has any identifying marks?"

"I never saw him. That's another question for Garren. I assume he, I mean Mudd the rabbit, not Garren…I assume he has long fur like the other rabbits. They're angoras. And the ones still in the rabbitry are mostly a bluish gray color, some lighter and some darker. Do you want to look at them so you have an idea what Mudd might look like?"

"Sure, let's do that. Maybe you could also look around in here and see if Ms. Woods has any photos of the rabbits."

"That's a good idea. I'm sorry I didn't think about it before. It was a little late when I got back here last night."

We got up. I grabbed the key Garren had left for the lock, and we went out to the rabbitry.

Officer Turner had behaved professionally the entire time he was asking me questions, looking at the rabbits, and taking a few pictures of the inside and outside of the shed and yard. We had just walked through the side gate, and he was moving towards his car when he stopped. He took a thin wallet out of his pocket and pulled out a business card. He walked back to me, took my hand and placed the card in it, then met my eyes.

"I am sorry it's a potential crime that's brought you back to town, but it's nice to see you again, Ms. Weber." He held my hand a beat longer and smiled.

"Th-thank you, Officer Turner," I stuttered. "I think."

"I told you before, call me Drew." He smiled wider. I could see flecks of brown in his green eyes. They held a little laughter as well.

"Drew," I said as I smiled back. "And call me Deana, please."

"Deana, like the Greek goddess."

"Hardly," I scoffed. My fingers went absently to my hair as I lowered my head, feeling my face warming in embarrassment.

He was still smiling as he got in his car and started the engine. He rolled the window down as he was backing up.

"Come by Town Hall later today or tomorrow and I'll have the report ready for you to sign. It's a few miles outside of the village, in Pekan Township. Goodbye, Deana." He called as he waved and drove off.

"Bye, Drew," I smiled and shook my head. I didn't think the man could help himself; flirting seemed to be a natural state for him.

After Drew left, I drove to the Sparrow to get breakfast. It was after ten and it looked like most of the customers were starting to come in for lunch. I ordered an egg salad sandwich with herb goat cheese and a large latte. As I was sitting at a table drinking my coffee and waiting for my sandwich, Gwen from Foxie Fibers walked in. She saw me and waved, then walked up to the pick-up area.

"Hi, Trini. I'm here for the B&B order," she said to Trinity, the owner of the Sparrow.

Trinity looked over from the display shelf where she was replacing some of the packaged foods the cafe sold.

"Ricky!" she hollered towards the back.

An older man came through the employee door leading to the back. He stood still and looked at Trinity but didn't say anything.

"Bring the B&B order up, please. Gwen's here for it."

Ricky gave a thumbs up and went back through the door. Trinity went back to stocking her shelves.

"Ricky doesn't say much," Gwen said as she came over and sat next to me. "He can talk just fine, but he doesn't like to. He's a little antisocial that way. He makes the best sandwiches though. Is that all you're having?" She pointed at my latte.

"No. I ordered an egg salad sandwich."

"With the herb cheese? That's delicious. You're going to love it."

She looked around the cafe and then back to me.

"Is someone meeting you here? Did your mom come with you this time?"

"No, it's just me."

"Then you have to come have lunch with me. I'm heading over to Emory's. He runs the Grey Fox Bed and Breakfast just past the church. He'll love meeting Stella's niece. Please, say you'll come."

"Um," I was about to turn her offer down, but she had such a hopeful look on her face. "Sure, why not."

"Great!"

Just then my order was called out. I went up to the pick-up counter and took my takeout carton just as Ricky came back through with a small box. He handed it to Gwen. She said goodbye to him and Trinity and then had me follow her outside. I told her I'd follow her over so I could leave from there. She shrugged and got in her car, going very slowly as she pulled out of her parking space and started driving down the road.

She took the first left and drove past a church on the corner. Behind it was a small graveyard with a short rock wall around it. I glanced over at the headstones. They looked old and weathered. Most of them probably dated to the beginning of the village, probably to the beginning of the country. I loved history and wanted to stop, get out and walk among them, reading the names and dates, and thinking of how this little village must have looked then; instead, I kept following Gwen, sipping my latte as I drove. She was still driving slow enough that I could have jogged beside her. We drove through a residential area. The road ended and we had to take a left. The B&B was a few yards up on the right.

The building looked like an old stone farmhouse, though it was obvious that someone had lovingly restored it. The stone looked clean and well maintained. The roof was a deep burgundy metal, and the roof of the stoop was a lightly weathered copper. There was deep green trim around all of the windows. We drove past it and parked in a graveled parking area on its left side. I finished the last of my latte, and grabbed my takeout carton, meeting Gwen as she walked towards the flagstone path leading to the double front doors.

We walked into the B&B, and I had to stop a moment to admire all of the wood trim and paneling. Whoever had decorated had been a lover of old English manor houses.

Gwen hollered, "Em, I've brought a guest," as we walked into the dining room and set the food down on a table.

"As long as I get my Reuben you can bring whomever you want," a voice answered. I assumed it was Gwen's friend Emory.

He walked into the dining room, wiping his hands on a kitchen towel.

"Emory Sullivan, meet Deana Weber. She's Stella's niece," Gwen said as she pulled food cartons out of her box and set them out on the table.

Emory looked over at me, raised his very bushy eyebrows and then walked over and took my hand. He looked about fifty-ish and seemed to define the quintessential proprietor of an inn, with a herringbone sweater vest and tasseled loafers.

"I am delighted to meet you, Deana Weber. And," he continued as he reached for one of the take-out cartons, "I will be more delighted if Trini remembered my extra sauerkraut. You two sit down. I'll be right back with something for us to drink. I hope lemonade is fine for everyone. I need to restock the juice and soda."

He walked out of the room, and I sat down.

Gwen sat and opened her carton.

"Emory and his husband started this place," she said quietly. "He lost him a few years ago. Heart attack."

I nodded that I understood, though I wasn't completely sure I did understand why she had told me. I opened my carton. The egg salad was spilling out of the sides of the bread. Luckily, Emory not only brought drinks when he came back in, he also had three sets of forks and knives, all on a pretty, distressed-wood tray.

"Ricky always overfills the sandwiches," Emory said knowingly as he set the tray down and handed me a knife and fork.

"Thank you," I said.

"Is lemonade alright, or would you like water?"

"Lemonade is fine," I said. He poured us each a glass and then sat down.

"Let's eat!" he said excitedly as he rubbed his hands together.

We all dug into our food, each making little sighs of pleasure. After he had eaten almost half of his sandwich, Emory wiped his mouth, took a drink and then looked over at me.

He smiled as he said, "I'm sure anyone you've spoken to can tell you that your aunt was a treasure. I personally will always consider meeting her a gift from the Divine." He held his palms facing up as he raised his eyes to the ceiling.

Gwen looked over at me, smiling with her eyes as she continued to eat. I had the feeling that she had heard Emory say that many times before.

"She actually met my husband, Jackson, first," he continued. "They were both at the Cardiac Center in Hershey for appointments. I wasn't there that day, but Jackson told me afterward that he had met this cute, silly, and lovely lady. It was Stella."

He took another bite of his sandwich as he appeared to be remembering the moments he was talking about. After a bit he cleared his throat and then yelled, "Stella!"

I jumped. Gwen's eyes went wide and then she started giggling. I gave a little nervous laugh and looked at Emory. He had a big smile on his face.

"He would yell her name every single time that she came over, just like Marlon Brando in *A Streetcar named Desire*." He chuckled, then reached for his glass.

"That was about ten years ago. The first time they met," he explained. "Jackson must have mentioned to her during their chat that we ran a B&B in Fox Cove, and the next thing you know Stella Woods is on our reservation list. She stayed overnight that time, on her way to a conference in Pittsburgh, I think."

"I hadn't met her yet," Gwen said to me. I think she was already living here when she came into my shop. That was about four or five years ago." She started to laugh again. "Remember, Em, I told you about meeting her?"

He smiled and nodded his head.

Gwen looked back at me, placing her hand on my arm. "Your aunt came in one day with a stack of shirt boxes full of wool, all neatly collected and labeled. She said she had more boxes in her car; all of this rabbit fur and couldn't give a hoot about knitting. She asked if I would want it. Do you believe it? Beautiful blue angora wool, almost five pounds of it and she wanted to just give it away!"

I looked at her and shrugged. "What was she supposed to do with it?"

"Why, sell it, silly! It's a process, taking that raw wool and turning it into yarn, but that yarn is worth quite a bit; some of the priciest yarn available."

"I didn't know that," I said. "I know angora sweaters are supposed to be expensive, but isn't there some animal rights thing about it being bad?"

"Anything can be exploited," Emory said. "Look at chickens. Fifty years ago no one was thinking of where their eggs came from. Now it's open range, non-GMO, pasture raised. And tuna. That's another food source that's been abused, but there's honest fishermen as well who get hurt by the bad press." He shrugged. "There are good ways of doing business and bad ways."

Gwen nodded. "Yes, but don't worry. Any angora wool and yarn that I carry is vetted by me as being humanely harvested. My suppliers know me personally and I verify that they keep clean and healthy rabbitries. There's quite a lot in the country and many in other countries. The ones I do business with are the small hobbyists or artisanal farms. Most spin and use their own yarn, but if they have excess, they sell it to shops like mine. My suppliers keep anywhere from ten to fifty rabbits, and they love them. There's quite a few who don't ever travel because they don't trust others to care for their bunnies."

"Huh," I said, getting interested in the topic. I had always enjoyed working reference at the library because helping patrons look up topics exposed me to new things. The hard part about the job was providing the service without appearing judgmental about the topics. It could be a very fine line depending on how strange the topic was, but I believed that libraries should be a place of learning that wasn't limited to a specific viewpoint or ideology. "I thought angora was like cashmere and came from goats," I mused.

"No, angora is from rabbits. There is mohair, which is similar, and that's from goats. You should come by the shop sometime. I'll give you a quick fiber lesson."

"That would be nice." I said.

"How are Stella's rabbits doing?" Gwen asked.

"Yes, how are they?" Emory also asked me. "Wasn't that young man from the veterinary clinic helping her with them?"

"Garren Hewett. Yes, he's still coming over. That's why I'm back in town, actually. One of Aunt Stella's rabbits was stolen."

Gwen and Emory both looked shocked.

"Oh, no!" Gwen said. "That's awful."

"Terrible," Emory agreed, "just terrible. Who would do such a thing?"

"I don't know. We called Officer Turner when I got in town last night."

"Who's 'we'? You said your mom wasn't here with you. Did you bring a boyfriend?" Gwen asked. I was realizing that as sweet as Gwen Fauks was, she also had a sharp mind for gossip.

"No boyfriend," I answered. "Just Garren. He came over to talk about the missing rabbit. He was the one who found it gone when he came over to care for them. We had dinner and then called his cousin, Officer Turner, to report the missing rabbit as stolen."

"You had dinner?" Emory said. "Anything good?"

"Uh, you," Gwen said, rolling her eyes. "You're always thinking with your stomach." Emory shrugged.

"It was good," I admitted. "He brought take-out from The Drake. He said his parents run it."

"Mm, yes," Emory said. "Their brandied pear *brasillé* is delicious. Jackson always ordered it when we ate there, sometimes before the main course."

Emory's eyes began to sparkle with tears. Gwen took his hand and gave it a squeeze. Growing uncomfortable, I started to pick up some of the containers and utensils.

"I'll start cleaning this up. Is the kitchen back there?" I asked, pointing to the doorway that Emory had gone back and forth through earlier. He nodded, and Gwen mouthed 'thank you' to me. I took the things I had gathered and walked back to the kitchen, dropping the cartons into the trash and putting the utensils in the sink. My phone began ringing where I had left it on the table just as I was walking back into the dining room.

It was Garren's number.

"Hello?"

"Deana, hi. It's Garren."

"Yes?"

"I wanted to let you know that I met with Drew. He's got my statement now. I was thinking of going to a place in the village that might have some information. Would you like to come with me?"

I thought about it.

"Sure. I'm in the village already. Give me the address and I'll meet you." I hung up after Garren gave me the name of an antiques store in the village. When I told Gwen and Emory that I had to leave, she gave me directions to the store. It was just around the corner and down another street. I thanked them both and hurried out.

CHAPTER TEN

I MET GARREN IN FRONT of Fuhsaz's Literary Emporium and Antiquities.

"That is a serious business name," I said as I walked up to him on the sidewalk.

"Gus is nothing if not pretentious."

"You don't like him?"

"There are just some people who rub you the wrong way. For me, that's Augustus Davies."

We walked into the store. Putting aside Garren's obvious dislike of the owner, I couldn't help being impressed. There were beautifully displayed antiques and many shelves of books, quite a few of them leather bound.

"May I help you? Oh, it's only you, Garren." A man said as he walked up to us.

"Hello, Gus" Garren said dryly.

The man ignored Garren. "And who is this? Hello. Augustus Davies at your service."

"Hi. I'm Deana Weber."

"Well, Miss Weber. What may I do for you today?"

"I'm not sure," I said. I looked at Garren quizzically, then looked past him. I saw a beautiful bookcase, with etched glass doors and carved scroll work along the front corners and on the faces of the two drawers below the enclosed shelving.

"That's beautiful," I heard myself saying. It seemed disrespectful to ignore such a beautiful piece of furniture. "Is it walnut?"

"You have a good eye, and very good taste. It's black walnut, about two hundred years old. The case was originally owned by a sea captain in Massachusetts."

"I'm a librarian. I'm around books a lot, and personally love them. I can just imagine it filled with leather bound classics."

"A noble career. I wish this country took as much care of its libraries as it does its sports stadiums. It might do the rabble some good."

I saw Garren roll his eyes.

"You might also like these," Gus said to me. He picked up one piece of a set of bookends and handed it to me. "They're from the same estate, bronze base with carved kauri wood."

I took the bookend and looked at the carving. It was a chunky piece of wood with multiple plant leaves carved into it in the shape of palm leaves or ferns. "It's very beautiful," I said as I traced the edges of the carving with my fingers. I handed it back to him carefully.

"The plant is a silver fern leaf," he explained. "It's a symbol of strength and power in New Zealand. The wood is the much-coveted ancient kauri. It's old wood that's been buried and can still be used after it's been dug up. It's very desirable. These beauties are only three fifty for the set," Gus said. "But I'll take another 10 percent off since you work in an academic field."

"I appreciate that," I said as I swallowed my sticker shock, "but I really can't right now."

"That's too bad." He placed the bookend back on the shelf right next to the other one.

"Had any interesting dishes lately, Gus?" Garren asked, breaking into the discussion.

"What are you going on about?"

"You know, some escargot, lamb stew, hasenpfeffer brisket, maybe?"

"I did try your father's *lapin au cidre* last fall. I must admit I was pleasantly surprised. It was almost as good as the original Normandy dish. I do hope he brings it back, if only for the season. Why are you asking?"

"And what about your personal cooking? Everyone in the village knows you like to cook with more than just beef and chicken."

"It's true. What of it? Have you grown so boring in your eating habits, Garren, that you can't enjoy an occasional dish of venison or pheasant? I swear, the fast-food epidemic in this country has deadened the American palette to anything that doesn't resemble a cheeseburger or chicken nugget."

Garren ignored Gus's condescending remark.

"There's a rabbit missing. Stolen," Garren said. "Would you know anything about that?"

"Why would I? I don't steal. I have no need to. My hunting club provides me with sport and fare for my table, and there's a supplier in the Midwest who keeps my freezer stocked with very high-quality meat. I have some delicious bison in there right now. What rabbit was stolen, exactly?"

"One of Stella's angoras."

"Ah, and you think because Ms. Woods and I didn't get along that I would stoop to taking one of her prize pets?" Augustus sneered.

"That's a little too petty for me, Garren. I gave up childish behavior in elementary school."

"Fine, Gus," Garren said. He shook his head. "Sorry to bother you. Would you let us know if you hear anything? My cousin, Drew Turner, is the officer handling the theft. Just call him."

Augustus didn't respond to Garren, just raised an eyebrow and gave him a haughty look. Then he turned back to me.

"It was lovely to meet *you*, Ms. Weber. Come back if you're still interested in the bookcase. I'm sure we can work something out."

I shook the hand he held out to me and followed Garren out the door.

We walked back outside to our cars.

"Do you really think that man could have had something to do with it?" I asked.

Garren pursed his mouth and looked at the ground.

"Not really," he admitted as he shrugged, "but I always have the feeling that Gus Davies knows more about the shady side of things. That snotty, upper-class act he walks around playing just seems too practiced, like he's behaving the way he thinks a..." he waved his hand around.

"A snotty, upper-class person would act?" I finished.

He shrugged again. "Yeah."

"What were all the questions about cooking and meats? You don't think Mudd was stolen for that, do you?" I almost choked on the words. I knew in my head that the steak, chicken, and ham, along with other meat came from animals. But those animals were raised on farms. Stella didn't run a farm, and her rabbits, from what I had seen, weren't being raised for food.

"I don't know," Garren said. "It's doubtful. The FDA has pretty strict guidelines for that if it's a business." I frowned and crossed my arms as I looked at him, still waiting for an explanation.

He threw his hands up in the air.

"I'm just trying to help, OK? I don't feel right just sitting around waiting to hear what's happened to Mudd. He was *my* responsibility."

His breath hitched a little and I realized he was really upset. I rubbed his arm, trying to soothe him.

"It's OK, Garren. I don't blame you," I said.

"I told Stella I'd take care of her rabbits. She trusted me. It's the last thing I said to her."

I squeezed his arm a little to get him to look at me.

"We'll find him," I said. "This isn't your fault. Stella would understand that."

He nodded that he'd heard me.

"I better go. I need to run a few errands before I go back to groom the rabbits and feed them."

"Maybe I could help with that," I said. "It wouldn't hurt for me to learn some of their care, would it?"

"Sure. We could do that. Give me a couple of hours."

"I'll see you later, then."

We each got in our cars. He waved at me as he pulled away, though he still looked sad.

I started my car and began to drive away but then realized that I had no idea where the Town Hall was. I put the car back in park, googled the address and typed it into the GPS. It was about seven miles outside of the village, in Pekan Township.

As I crossed the bridge on the road out of town, I saw the fancy, blue Tesla driving towards me, heading into the village. The man behind the wheel had on dark glasses and held what looked like an electronic cigarette to his mouth. I thought of the sticker on the back window and wondered if what he was smoking was something stronger. Less than ten minutes later I had parked and was walking through the doors of Pekan Town Hall.

CHAPTER ELEVEN

I PARKED AND WALKED into the building, asking for Officer Turner. I was directed to an office towards the back of the central hallway. I walked in and immediately saw Drew sitting at a desk, hunched over the pile of papers in front of him. Another officer approached me, and I said I was meeting Officer Turner, pointing towards him.

"Hey, Turner," the officer hollered.

Drew looked up, squinting my way. I saw his face relax as he refocused on me and away from whatever he had been reading. He stood up and walked over to me, reached out and opened the waist high swinging door that separated the public area of the office from the official area, and waved me through.

"Glad you made it in, Deana."

"Sorry it's later than I thought. I got a little sidetracked."

"No problem. Let's get this report wrapped up."

He sat back down at his desk after dragging a chair over from another area for me to sit in. He shuffled through a few folders and then pulled one out, squinting his eyes again as he read something off of the page.

"Here you go," he said as he put the typed report down in front of me. "Look this over and let me know if it's complete or if I've left anything out, then I'll have you sign. Here's a pen."

He handed me a pen and I looked down to read the report. It looked like it included everything, even a detailed description of Mudd. He must have gotten that information from Garren since I hadn't had a chance to go back to the house and look through any files yet for records or pictures of the rabbits.

"It looks good to me," I said. I signed and handed the forms back to him.

"Good. I'll be questioning people in the area. Hopefully we'll have some news for you soon. Just remember, this isn't TV. These things take time in real life."

"I understand. And you can probably skip talking to at least one person, Mr. Davies, at Fuhsaz's. We spoke to him earlier and he..."

Drew leaned forward in his chair. "What do you mean, 'we spoke to him'?"

I leaned back a little, feeling like I was about to be reprimanded. "Um, I mean me and Garren."

"And why would you go speak to Mr. Davies about your missing rabbit, Deana?"

"Garren thought he might know something. I guess Gus — Mr. Davies — knows farmers that provide specialty or game meats for sale, and he thought if someone stole Mudd to sell to a meat breeder then Mr. Davies might have heard about it."

Drew flopped back in his chair, pushing his hand through his hair. I hadn't noticed before, but he had some gray strands peppering the light brown hair just above his ears.

"You can't just go around questioning people, Deana. This is an active investigation. What if Mr. Davies does know something? Now that you two have talked he'll know the police won't be far behind, but when we go talk to him, he'll have a story prepared, or have gotten rid of any evidence if he had it."

"Oh, well, I think Garren was just trying to help. We were just trying to help," I explained weakly. "He feels so bad about Mudd being stolen. He feels like he let Stella down."

"And that's why he should stay out of it. He's too emotionally involved." He looked at me and pointed his finger. "And you stay out of it too. If you want to help, then get me a photo of this rabbit. The details I have are from the vet records, but there's no picture. That would help."

"I will. I'm heading back to the house from here. I'll start looking through Stella's files when I get there."

He showed me out of the office and back down the hall to the front of the building, waving me off as he opened the door. I walked down the steps and back to my car. I felt thoroughly chastised and told myself I would do what he wanted, which was almost nothing. I just hoped Garren would feel the same way.

I GOT BACK TO STELLA'S house by late afternoon.

I went through her file drawers in the study. Stella, thankfully, was meticulous about keeping her papers and files in order. The research librarian in me was secretly proud of her. It wasn't in the files that I finally found what I was looking for though. After thirty minutes of going through the study, I realized that I was looking at this the wrong way. Stella didn't just think of the rabbits as a business. The way Garren had described her with them meant that she loved them. I walked towards her bedroom door. It was still shut from the last time I was here. I opened it and stood in the doorway for a moment. I still felt like I was intruding on her space. After a moment I walked forward. The feeling didn't go away, but I told myself that it was for a good reason. I was trying to find Mudd.

"Sorry, Aunt Stella," I said to the empty room anyway.

I moved around the room, seeing the daily things that were personal to a woman I wish I had taken the time to know better.

I found the albums tucked onto a shelf with various statues of rabbits. One album was the usual collection of personal photos. I flipped through them, watching as pieces of Stella's life connected one to the other in frozen moments. I set the book aside, planning to take it with me so I could show it to my mom when I saw her. The other album had what I was looking for. It was full of various pictures of the rabbits, each one tagged with a sticker that included their name and age when the photo was taken. Mudd's pictures were at the front of the album. I took one out that showed him in the rabbit pen. It was from a few years ago. His black head and ears were facing the camera and completely surrounded by the fluffy bluish gray fur on his body. He had a green leaf in his mouth that he must have been nibbling on when Stella took the picture. She had zoomed in so close to take the shot that I could see the color variations on the strands of his fur.

I took the albums and the photo into the living room, set the photo down and took a picture of it with my phone, then sent it to the cell number on Drew's business card. Just as I finished my phone rang. Lilli was calling me.

"Hello," I said.

"Just thought I'd check on you. My three o'clock canceled so I have some free time. What have you been up to today?"

"Well, let's see, I've been chewed out by Officer Turner, although he still managed to flirt with me before that. I've tried to reassure Garren that it's not his fault that the rabbit was stolen, and I've learned that Americans eat too much boring fast-food."

"Wow, that's quite a list of accomplishments," Lilli said.

"I have no idea what I'm doing here. It feels wrong to just wait, but that's what I've been told to do. I think I might need to stay a few more days."

"How about I come wait with you, at least for the weekend? I was going to babysit the kids while Rose and Franklin went out on Saturday, but Becca has pink eye, so they're all staying home, and I'm staying away. I could drive over tomorrow after work, and I can bring you extra clothes."

"That would be great, Lilli. Although, I should warn you, I've been sleeping on the couch. It just feels weird in her bedroom. I only walked in here today to look for photos of the rabbits, for the police."

"Deana," Lilli said. She had taken on her 'therapy' voice and I knew she was going to say something about grief and blah, blah, blah.

"I know, Lilli," I said.

"Well, we'll work on those emotional walls when I get there. Do you have the appropriate supplies, or should I bring some?"

I knew she meant food, and of course wine.

"I'll take care of it. There's a small grocery store here and I think I saw a wine shop."

"Great! Then I'll see you tomorrow. And Deana?"

"Wha-at?" I drawled.

"Find some sheets and strip the bed. Because I'm not sleeping on a couch." She hung up. I stared at the phone, frowning at it as if it had personally offended me. Then I looked towards the hallway that led back to the bedroom.

"I'll do that tomorrow."

I put the rabbit photo away and took the photo album back to the room. I was about to shut the door again, but I stopped. I moved it back to a position that left it half open, and half closed.

See, I thought, *I could deal with emotional walls.*

When I heard Garren pull up to the house I met him outside the rabbitry. He unlocked the door and went inside, turning on the lights. He shut the door once I was inside.

"Couldn't we just leave the door open for some fresh air," I asked.

"Only if you want to chase rabbits around for the rest of tonight," he said. He smiled back at me as he stepped over the short barrier.

"Just because these are domestic animals doesn't mean they listen. It would be like leaving a gate open and expecting a horse to still be in the corral."

"Got it," I said.

"Thursdays are grooming and play days, Sundays too. I start with the ladies on the right and work my way around to the boys. Some of them play nice together so I'll let them out in groups. But we never let the boys out with other boys. They fight too much. And only let a boy out with girls if they've been fixed or else there will be *a lot* of little unplanned baby bunnies running around. Could you reach down on the wall in front of the shelf and lift the door?"

He pointed to the wall at the end of the row of hutches. I walked back and, sure enough, there was a small pet door that had been added to the side of the shed. I lifted out the plastic insert so that there was only a clear, thin rubber flap over the opening.

He opened one of the hutches and took out the rabbit. Her fur caught the light overhead. The soft blue-gray fibers looked like waves on a stormy seashore.

"Hello, Bessie. How's my girl today?" He held her close to his body with one hand while he rubbed her head lightly. Then he walked over to the pet door and set her down in front of it. Her nose twitched for a moment, then she stepped forward a little. In the next instant she had disappeared through the door. I remembered that outside the rabbitry was a wire enclosed area.

"Here," Garren said. I turned around and he was handing me a rabbit. "This is Fleetsie."

I held my arms out without thinking. "I can't...I don't..."

"Just relax. Put one arm around her middle and stroke her head softly with the other. They're very sensitive animals so just try to calm yourself."

I did what he said. "Hi, little lady," I whispered. "You're the cutest thing I've ever seen." Her fur tickled my nose, and I felt myself smiling. "What do I do now?" I whispered to Garren.

He laughed. "Put her down in front of the door. She knows where she wants to go."

I sat her down and watched as she disappeared through the pet door even faster than Bessie.

Garren took another rabbit out. Rainey. She also went through the little door. He took one more rabbit out and set her on the floor.

"Close the door now, and then hand me the white bin behind you with the brushes and blower."

I set the plastic back in the slot and then handed him a bin off the shelf. It had four compartments with a handle in the center. Each section held either brushes, scissors and clippers, or the thing I assumed was the blower, with tubes in the last compartment. He was setting up a small folding table in the center of the space. After he got the table up, he plugged in the blower and attached a tube to it. It looked like a child-sized vacuum cleaner. When the rabbit hopped near him, he scooped her up, petting her and talking to her as he placed her on the table. "Hey, Ella, let's get you fixed up." He started blowing the air on her fur, moving it methodically over her body. I thought she would have tried to get away, but she barely moved, just hunkered down as the air moved over her. He shut the blower off and took a brush out of the bin, brushing her fur and removing any clumped pieces.

"So, do you cut all of their hair off with the scissors after this?" I asked, remembering Gwen's story from lunch about Stella bringing in her boxes of angora wool.

"Not yet, and I'll probably be plucking it instead of cutting it. I'll start that in a few weeks. If you're still here," he said and looked over at me, "I'll show you how to do it, if you're interested."

"Does it hurt them?"

"No, the fur that gets removed is already loose, but their fur grows so closely together and is so fine that it doesn't always disconnect on its own. They actually remind me of one of our client's dogs, a Cairn terrier. It's called hand-stripping with dogs, but it's a similar process. A lot of terrier breeds are hand-stripped instead of cut or shaved because of their dual coats and the way the colors of those layers grow in."

He put Ella back in her hutch, then took out Joplin, and then Billie Bee, grooming each of them after letting them run around on the floor for a little while. I sat on the floor while they were loose and reached out to gently pet them whenever they came close to me.

"It seems like an odd pet to me, but I can kind of see why Stella liked them."

"They can be a lot of work, but yes, they're special. Why don't you come up here and try the blower with Billie. She's pretty docile." He motioned me up. I got up off the floor, brushing my hands off, then attempted to brush the rabbit fur off of my clothes.

"You may as well quit. It's got a life of its own. I'm constantly cleaning out my truck seats from where it's traveled home with me. Stella should have lint rollers in her house if you want to clean up when we're done."

I stopped trying to get the fur off and stood next to him as he showed me how to keep a constant motion of the blower on the rabbit and use my free hand to stay ready to grab her if she decided to jump off of the table. After I was done blowing out her coat and then brushing her, she looked like a fluffy gray cloud. I had the urge to bury my face in her fur and rub it back and forth like a child with a security blanket. I resisted though and handed her off to Garren to put her back in her hutch.

Garren had me reopen the rabbit door and then he went out to the pen and coaxed them back through and into the rabbitry. Once they were all inside again, I closed the door. He came back inside and got them back in their hutches. Next, he let out Howler, Shemi, Ruthie, and Popi V. While those four were outside he refilled the food for all of the rabbits, then we switched the loose ones with Vaughan, which according to Garren, was the only breeding male in the rabbitry. He had to play by himself, so he didn't get frisky with the female rabbits. That left just HRH BB.

"What about him?" I asked, pointing to the rabbit where he still sat in his hutch.

"Oh, BB is special. He's not called 'His Royal Highness' only because he's named after BB King." Garren opened the hutch and coaxed BB out into the center of the rabbitry floor. "This guy thinks he's a royal. What he is, is a royal pain in the butt, aren't you, Your Highness?" He rubbed the rabbit behind his ears. BB hopped around a little and then plopped down on the mats, spreading his hind legs out so that his tummy was flat on the floor. Garren let him stay there for a second or two and then picked him up and set him on the grooming table. After he had blown his fur out and brushed him, he set him down to hop around a little more. BB hopped over to the rabbit door, sniffed it, and then peed on it.

Garren shook his head. "He does it every time. All the males do. That's why we have the barriers up between the boys' and girls' hutches, but BB's extra stubborn about marking. And he fights with everyone, boys and girls, so he doesn't get to play with them."

"That's sad. He must be lonely."

"You wouldn't feel so bad for him if you had seen him fighting with Howler. He drew blood. It was not a pretty sight."

Garren finally scooped up BB and set him back in his hutch. He cleaned off the rabbit door, then cleaned and put away the grooming supplies. He had me go outside to the pen and coax Vaughn back inside so that he could let BB outside for a little while. After we had gotten the last rabbits in and tucked away for the evening, we locked up the rabbitry.

"I'll groom the ones I didn't do today when I'm here on Sunday," Garren said as we stood on the flagstones.

"OK."

"I'm sorry again, about today. I just thought if Gus had heard anything that maybe he would tell us. He's not all bad."

I raised my eyebrows at him but didn't respond.

"Yes, I know. I didn't help with my 'attitude.'" He made air quotes. I tried to stop myself from smiling. He was feeling contrite, I could tell.

"Will you still let me help, please?" he asked.

"Of course, Garren. But let's let your cousin, Drew, help too. He is a cop, after all. I sent him a picture of Mudd, and he's got all of your information."

"Drew's good at his job," Garren conceded. "Don't tell him I said that."

I twisted an invisible key in my mouth. "Your secret is safe."

Garren finally smiled. He leaned over and gently pulled something from my hair, then brushed a strand away that had fallen in front of my cheek. "You had some angora in your hair," he explained, then awkwardly stepped back. "I'll see you Sunday, Deana. We'll have another grooming lesson if you're up for it."

"I'll see you here. Bye, Garren."

He waved and left through the garden gate.

I watched as he drove away, reaching up to brush my hair off my face again. I pushed away the slight flutter I felt in my stomach, deciding to contribute it to hunger pangs since it was close to dinner time.

CHAPTER TWELVE

FRIDAY MORNING WAS rainy.

After picking up around the house, mostly in the living room where I had been sleeping, I drove into the village, grabbed a latte and breakfast sandwich at the Sparrow, and then drove down the street. I parked in front of Tresser's Market since I was going there last, then walked across the street to the wine shop I had noticed before. Ada's Arbor looked plain from the outside. The building was two story brick with a large window at street level next to the front door and two windows on the second floor. A simple wood sign above the door had the name of the shop carved in the center of a picture of an arbor with what I assumed were grape vines hanging from it. I walked inside and was immediately surprised.

At the entrance I walked under a wood arbor that had been set up around the doorway. As I looked up, I saw fake grapevines that had been wrapped around the beams of the arbor. They trailed down on each side where they curled around wine bottle holders that had been attached to the sides of the arbor. Small baskets for shopping were stacked just outside of the arbor. The floor was plain, wide wood planks and almost every foot of it contained shelves full of bottles. There were also some bar accessories, glasses and linens mixed in with the bottles. On the ceiling I noticed more of the mobiles, like the ones that were hanging at the Sparrow Cafe.

I began browsing, happily losing myself in selecting a couple bottles of red. I also found a shelf full of craft beers, and then another section that had a glass front cooler full of smaller bottles. The pictures on the bottles drew me over. I was staring intently at them when a woman walked up to me.

"Do you drink mead?" she asked.

"I've never tried it," I admitted.

"Oh, you're in for a treat then. Let me give you a taste." She waved me over to a small tasting counter.

"It's sweeter than most wines, more of a dessert flavor. There's also a higher alcohol content. That's why the bottles are smaller than a wine bottle." She poured a small amount into a sample size glass and handed it to me.

"It's made from honey, not grapes, which is where the sweetness comes from," she said.

I took the glass and had a tentative sip. The liquid touched my lips. The light sweetness and fermentation of the liquid broke over my tongue. "Oh, wow, that's really good," I said. I finished the sample, tipping the glass high to catch every drop.

She laughed. "I think you like it."

I smiled. "Oh yes. What's the flavor, though? It tastes like more than honey."

She turned the bottle towards me that she had placed on the counter so that I could see the label.

"This one is Brigit's Elixir. It's got blueberry and some savory spices to balance out the sweetness. Brigit was a Gaelic goddess with many attributes, including hearth, fire, and inspiration. The meadery that makes this likes to use old world themes for their products."

"The label is beautiful."

"It is, I agree. Would you like to try another one?"

"I would, but I think I better not. I will take a bottle of this one though," I said, tapping the bottle of Brigit's Elixir.

"Lovely. I'm Ada, by the way, Ada Breene. I haven't seen you in here before."

"Oh, this is your shop!" I said as I connected her name to the store.

"Yes, it is."

"It's great. I wasn't expecting such a good selection in such a small village."

"Well, just because we're small doesn't mean we can't have good taste," she said cheerfully. "I'm very selective about my stock. I figure the more basic beer and wines can be bought at the grocery store. They have more space. People who come to me are looking for something a little different, a little more unique."

"And the mobiles? I noticed them at the cafe also. Are they a local artist?"

"Yes, Charley Perez. Aren't they great?"

"They are. They remind me of..."

"Being little?" she said, finishing my thought.

"Exactly," I said.

"She laughed again. "They always have that effect. He's very talented."

I agreed. She rang up my purchases and I promised I would come back soon. I set the bottles in my car, now thankful for the drizzly day since the temperature inside the car would stay cooler. I ran into the grocery store and got a few snacks and supplies. I was staring at frozen meals when I had the bright idea to get takeout from The Drake. It would be so much better than the frozen food I was looking at. I loaded the grocery purchases into my car and then walked back across the street to The Drake. Having all of these shops within walking distance was really convenient. I had bought wine, groceries, and a fully prepared meal all while being parked in one spot.

After getting back to the house I put the food and wine away, then hunted around for some sheets, finding some in Stella's bedroom closet. I quickly stripped and remade the bed, trying not to think about it too hard. I was fine with Lilli sleeping in Stella's room. I just didn't feel right being in there. I found a vacuum cleaner tucked into a corner of the study and ran it over the floors as well. Feeling like I had made enough of a cleaning effort I then went back to looking through the study. I had brought the files that Gladys Laine had left with me in here and stacked them on the desk. I set aside the ones I had already looked through and was moving the envelope that had held the keys when I realized it wasn't empty. I opened it and saw another envelope inside. I had completely forgotten about seeing it when I had taken the keys out.

Inside the envelope was a disc case. I opened it and read the handwritten label on the disc. It had Stella's name and a date on it from about six months ago. I read the disc description and realized that it was a DVD, not a CD, which meant it was most likely a video that Stella had made. I bit my lip as I contemplated watching it, then shut the case. I decided watching the video might be better done with company. I would wait until Lilli was here. I set it next to the TV in the living room and walked away.

WHEN LILLI GOT TO THE house, I had the wine open and lamb stew from The Drake keeping warm in a pot on the stove. The leftover bread was sliced, and the containers of herb butter were sitting out as well.

She was very impressed with the food.

While we ate I told her about finding the DVD and that I was waiting for her to arrive so she could watch it with me. We finished dinner and took our wine into the living room. I put the DVD in and hit play on the remote.

There were a few moments at the beginning that were a blank screen then it switched over to a view of Aunt Stella. She was sitting at what looked like her kitchen table. It was a shock to see her on the screen, even knowing that the DVD was going to be of her.

She began to talk.

"Hello? So, I guess I just start talking. Okay, here it goes. Hi, Celia, and Deana if you're here as well. If you're watching this then I suppose my life must be done. It's okay. I've known for a very long time that I was living on borrowed time. But I also know that I've lived my life as fully and authentically as possible. I've gone to so many places and seen so many wonderful things, met so many wonderful people. I don't have regrets, well, not many. There is one or two I guess." Stella got a faraway look in her eyes as she focused on something off camera.

But that's for later. Right now, there's all the business of life to deal with. I've tried to make this part as painless as possible. Celia, you know most of what I've done. You've got the deed to the house, and I've gifted amounts to Phillip and Lance. They're great boys. All your kids are great, and I'm so grateful that I was able to be a part of their lives, so grateful for having you in my life, Celia.

I haven't explained before now why I made you and Deana my beneficiaries. I wasn't playing favorites. Let's get that clear. It's more that I was upholding a tradition, one of the very few that I can remember from my own family, and since I don't have any blood relatives anymore, I've chosen you and Deana to carry on my tradition.

You see, in my family, the women have always left their personal property to any future female descendants. I don't know how it started. My grandmother told me once that she remembered her mother telling her that it was a birthright, and that any marriage was preceded by a contract stating that this birthright would be upheld. I suppose that in the past the normal way of leaving estates to the eldest son was not looked upon kindly by my female ancestors, and so they developed their own rule.

Knowing my independent streak, Celia, I'm sure you can see how much this idea appealed to me."

Lilli and I started laughing at Stella's comment, and at the kinship she felt towards her predecessors as we saw the apparent twinkle light up her eyes on the recording.

"That was definitely Aunt Stella's style," I said.

Lilli raised her wine glass to Stella's image. "I like how this lady thinks."

Stella continued more soberly.

"As to those regrets? I said there weren't many, but what life can be lived with none? Not mine it seems. One regret I have is, of course, involving a man. I met him a couple of years ago after moving to Fox Cove. We became friends, and then we became more. I introduced him to you, Celia. You remember, Gregory Martin? Well, it was good between us for quite a while, but then it wasn't. I know you've always been a little confused about why I got involved with keeping my rabbits. Let me just say now that if anything happens with them, especially Muddy Waters, that you should look for Gregory."

Stella's image froze and the DVD screen suddenly went blank. I stopped it, then turned to Lilli.

"Oh my God!" I cried and jumped up from the couch. "Do you know what this means?"

"Stella and Gregory were involved." Lilli mused.

"No! Well, yes. But not that. Stella said if anything happens to the rabbits, especially Mudd, that we should look at Gregory! Gregory must have taken Mudd!"

"Maybe, but she said look *for* Gregory, not *at* Gregory."

"Semantics," I said, waving away her doubt. "I should call the police, get them to go over to Gregory Martin's."

"Just slow down. You already confronted one person and got in trouble for it. You need to approach things better this time. Let's sleep on it tonight and then tomorrow you and I can pay a friendly visit to Gregory Martin. We'll say that, oh I don't know, Stella wanted him to have one of those rabbit figurines that are in her bedroom, or something like that. We can look around his place a little, see if anything looks suspicious, and then we can call the police."

She looked at me expectantly. I chewed my lip as I thought over her idea. It did make more sense.

I felt myself deflating a little. I sat back down. "OK. We can do that. I'll take you to the Sparrow Cafe for breakfast. I've seen Gregory there before so if he shows up then we can follow him back to his house."

"Perfect! Now," she held out my wine glass to me, "finish your wine, and then you can show me these bunnies that are causing so much trouble."

CHAPTER THIRTEEN

"I LOVE THESE MOBILES!" Lilli said for the third time as we sat in the Sparrow having breakfast.

"I think I'm going to buy one for Becca and Matthew. Maybe the one with the mix of birds and insects. It doesn't seem too cutesy. What do you think?"

"I like them all, but will the kids fight over it?" I looked up at the mobiles. They were cute and whimsical, but they were also art, and I'd hate to see them damaged.

"Hmm, good point. Maybe I should get two smaller ones. I'm going to go look around." She took her empty plate and coffee mug to the dish bin and then started walking around, looking at the hanging displays scattered around the cafe. I smiled as I watched her enjoying herself. As I finished my coffee I contemplated Stella's video recording. Her explanation about her family tradition of the women leaving their belongings to the next female generation had seemed odd and outdated, like primogeniture in the English aristocracy of past centuries. It started me thinking about castles and stone walls covered in tapestries.

"Having a good morning?" a voice said, breaking into my musings.

I looked up. Garren was standing next to the table, holding a covered coffee cup.

"Oh, Hi," I said.

"Hi." He smiled. "I asked if you were having a good morning."

"Yes, thanks. My friend, Lilli, came in for the weekend. She's around here somewhere." I started looking around. I spotted her across the cafe. She laughed and I looked at who was standing next to her. "It looks like Drew has met her already," I said as I nodded to where they were standing. Garren looked over at them and smiled.

"Yep, he definitely has a gift with women. But don't worry, he's not a bad guy. Even his exes still like him."

"Does he have a lot of exes?" I asked suspiciously.

"Uh, I'm going to quit talking now. He is my cousin."

I narrowed my eyes as I looked at him. Just then Lilli arrived back at our table, Drew trailing behind her.

"Deana, guess who I just met?" she said enthusiastically.

"Hey, Deana," Drew waved.

I waved back.

"Drew was telling me that he's the officer who came out when you thought Garren was a bear," Lilli said brightly. "Are you Garren?" she asked, looking at Garren.

"I am," he said.

"This is great! We should get together later. Maybe lunch? What do you think, De?"

"Uh, I'm sure they're busy." I said, trying to give Lilli the hint that I didn't want to. She ignored me.

"Nope," Garren said.

"Not really," Drew echoed. "I'll be on duty later, but I could swing by for lunch." He smiled at Lilli, his eyes twinkling. He looked over at me.

"Fine. Let's have lunch."

"Great!" Lilli said, clapping her hands. "De and I will pick up food. Come over around one."

Drew and Garren both accepted and said they would be there, then left.

"What was that?" I asked her as she sat back down.

"What?" she responded innocently.

"You want to have lunch with a couple of guys you don't even know?"

"You had dinner with Garren already. What's the big deal? And Drew's cute. You don't like him, do you?"

"No. I mean, yes, he's a nice guy, but I don't have a 'thing' for him."

"Perfect. And it's also perfect because you can tell them both about the video."

"You're kind of devious, Lilli Hughes."

She smirked. "Let's go walk around a little. You can show me the village before we pick up lunch."

I took my dishes up to the bin and we left, going by Gwen's store, Foxie's, where Gwen welcomed Lilli just as enthusiastically as she had me, minus the condolences. We were able to slip out shortly after thanks to another customer who needed help. Lilli wasn't in the mood for books or antiques, so we got in the car and drove the short distance to the market and wine shop. After picking out a bottle of wine and another bottle of mead, which we both enjoyed having a tasting of, we went to Tresser's Market and picked up fixings for an easy lunch, chicken and green apple sausage brats and potato salad, with a strawberry cheesecake for dessert. We also bought tea bags and sugar to make a pitcher of iced tea.

After putting the food away for later, we realized that we didn't have a lot to do. We decided to take a walk. We strolled down the driveway. Trees were swaying in a light breeze. Birds zipped back and forth. We walked along the road.

"We could never do this in the city," Lilli said as she tightrope-walked the line down the center of the road.

"Nope," I agreed, "at least three cars would have run you over by now."

"So how long do you think you'll be here?"

"I guess until this silly rabbit is found."

"And then what?"

"What do you mean? Then I go back home and find a job."

A LITTLE BEFORE ONE Garren drove up. Drew arrived right after, already changed into his uniform. We sat at the kitchen table eating and chatting. I had to pull an extra chair in from the study. Drew and Lilli were having a discussion about psychology practices in law enforcement.

"Criminal psychology was part of my education, but I didn't really feel a connection to it," Lilli said. I'm drawn more to family dynamics."

"Sometimes those family dynamics can lead to criminal behavior," Drew countered.

"That's true. Do you have much interaction with the..." Drew's phone went off on his hip. He excused himself and walked into the living room.

"So Garren," Lilli continued, switching effortlessly to him, "what do you like most about your work with animals?"

"Um," Garren covered his mouth and mumbled, trying to finish chewing the food he had in his mouth.

"Lilli," I admonished, "let him eat, geesh."

"It's OK," Garren said finally. He took a drink of his tea and then answered Lilli's question. "I like animals. I like helping them, and helping people take care of them."

Lilli eyed him with a straight face, then nodded. "You're a very uncomplicated person, aren't you?"

Garren shrugged. "I guess I am."

Drew walked back. "Sorry, I've gotta run. They need me to come in a little early. Deana, Lilli, thanks for lunch. I'll look forward to seeing you both again soon." We said goodbye to him and finished our meal.

WE HAD FINISHED CLEANING up the lunch dishes, and Lilli was just taking out the cheesecake that we had bought for dessert when there was a knock on the door. When I opened it Drew was standing there.

"You're back," I said smiling at him. I waited for one of his flirty comments, but he just gave me a serious nod.

"Can I come in?"

"Of course," I stepped aside to let him in, feeling confused by his behavior, then shut the door. He stood in the living room. Lilli and Garren came in from the kitchen with three plates of cheesecake.

"Oh, hey, Drew," Garren said. "You want some dessert?"

"Actually, I need to speak with Deana."

"About what?" I asked.

"You said that you and Lilli stopped at Fuhsaz's Literary Emporium and Antiquities on Thursday?"

"Yes. I told you we did."

"Have you gone back there since?"

"No, why?"

Drew had his hands resting on his belt. He was tapping it nervously, then he reached up and rubbed the back of his head. He finally looked at me again, sighed and spoke. "Augustus Davies was found dead this afternoon."

"Oh my God!" Lilli and I both said at once.

"Drew, why are you acting so weird?" Garren asked.

Drew ignored him and continued to look at me.

"Why are you looking at me like that?" I asked.

"Did you touch anything while you were there?"

"I don't think so. No, wait, I did. Mr. Davies handed me a bookend, one of a set. He offered me a discount on it but the price was still too much for me."

"Was it metal and wood, with some kind of plant carving on it?"

"Yes, from New Zealand, I think he said."

Drew pursed his lips. "Well, that bookend was used to hit Mr. Davies. Cracked his skull open."

I sunk onto the couch, setting aside the plate Lilli had handed me.

"Oh, no," I whispered.

"Your prints were found on it, Deana. Just yours, and Mr. Davies's."

"Well, this is ridiculous," Lilli said. "You're acting like you think Deana did it."

"I do need you to make a statement, answer some questions."

"You're not serious?" Lilli said.

"You are serious," I said, looking at his face.

"Drew, come on man. There's no way she did this," Garren said.

"I'm not saying she did, Garren, but this has to be done. It's procedure."

"It's OK, guys. Let's just get this over with." I stood up.

"I'll drive you in and bring you back when we're done," Drew said.

"Lilli, could you…"

"Don't worry, Deana. I'll be here. If you're not back in two hours I'm calling your dad, and a lawyer." She gave me a hug. She gave Drew a hard look, then stomped away from him, going to stand beside Garren and crossing her arms.

CHAPTER FOURTEEN

"DO YOU RECOGNIZE THIS object, Ms. Weber?" the officer asked me.

My hand flew to my mouth as I looked down at the photo she slid in front of me on the table.

I was back at the Town Hall in Pekan Township, in a small room. It was nicer than the cold, ugly concrete interrogation rooms that I had seen on cop shows, but I still felt uncomfortable.

"Is that blood?" I asked.

I met her eyes, and she raised an eyebrow as if to say, *Of course it's blood. What were you expecting, strawberry syrup?*

I dropped my hand and took a breath. "Yes, it's a bookend."

My voice came out hoarse and I cleared my throat before repeating myself. "It's a bookend. One of a set. Gus, I mean Mr. Davies, showed it to me on Thursday when I was in his store."

"Did you hold the bookend that day?" the officer asked.

"Yes. He handed it to me to look at the plant carving in the wood."

"Can you point out where the bookend was before he handed it to you?"

She slid another photo on the table. It showed a broader view of the store. The shelf where Gus had taken the bookend from was to one side of the photo frame. I could just see a corner of the bookcase that I had admired on the opposite side, and right in the center, on the floor, was Augustus Davies. He was lying on his side, one arm thrown over his body and one arm raised above his head. I said a silent prayer that he was facing away from the photographer. I couldn't see whatever wound the bookend had made, but I did see a dark, wet puddle on the floor around his head. I made an involuntary choking sound and pushed away from the table. When I met the officer's eyes again, she was looking at me, her head tilted to one side and an expression of curiosity on her face.

I got mad.

"You did that on purpose."

"What?" she said innocently.

I shook my head, refusing to play in to the tactics. Even if my dad hadn't been a cop, I had watched enough TV shows and movies to know she was gauging my reaction to seeing the body.

I poked my finger at the shelf. "It was here, next to the other one."

"Right next to it? Weren't there books in between? That is what bookends are for, to hold books."

"No," I said. "They were up against each other, no books in between, and he put them back that way also."

She gave me a long look, then sat back. She set a pad in front of me. "Write down your contact information, please. And thanks for your time."

She gathered the photos together, got up and walked out of the room. I wrote down my phone number and my address in Philadelphia as well as Stella's address. Drew came in as I was setting the pen down on the pad.

"Are you ready to go?" he asked.

I sighed heavily, stood up, and pushed in my chair. "Are they done grilling me?"

"That wasn't grilling," he said and smiled. I didn't smile back, and his smile slowly dissolved.

"Deana," he put his hand on my shoulder, "this was just fact gathering. We need to recreate a timeline: who was there and when, where things were at what time. It's just part of the process."

"It's a very uncomfortable process," I muttered.

"It's a murder investigation. Would you want to be comfortable with that?"

"Just let me pout, Officer Turner," I said and walked past him.

I didn't wait to hear his comment. He caught up with me outside and we got back in his car.

I knew in my head that I was being petty by not talking to him on the drive back to Stella's. It wasn't his fault. He was just doing his job. Still, I needed the time to *process* the murder process.

I finally felt a little less anxious as we parked in front of Stella's. As I got out, I turned back and said, "I'm not mad at you, just at the situation."

He gave a nod. "I get it."

"And, Deana," he called as I was opening the front door. I turned back and looked at him.

"Don't leave town," he said, gave me a big smile and then drove away.

My mouth dropped open. *He can't be serious*, I thought. *Can he?*

Lilli was waiting for me. She had cleaned up from lunch and was listening to some of Stella's music. She jumped up from where she was sitting and rushed over to me.

"Are you OK?"

"I'm alright." I sighed and sank onto the couch.

"Want some wine?" I gave her a baleful look. "Of course you want some wine. Be right back."

She came back from the kitchen a few minutes later with wine and a slice of cheesecake that I hadn't gotten to eat earlier.

"Thanks, Lilli." I took a bite, but it tasted like cardboard. I set the plate aside and picked up my drink. I stared into my wine glass as I sloshed the liquid around. "I feel like I have a huge cloud over me, like a big, dark swirling vortex of crap."

"Like a hurricane?"

"More like a tornado, just tossing me around and throwing my life in multiple directions." I threw my hand up in the air and spun it around for effect.

"Very dramatic." Lilli said. "So, to change that depressing subject, when are you going to tell Garren about the video?"

I swirled my wine and then took a sip. I didn't want to tell Garren. I didn't want a repeat of what happened with Gus. What if he had a problem with Gregory Martin as well? I really didn't need *more* drama.

"Probably in the morning. He'll be over to feed the rabbits."

I didn't mention that I might leave before I saw him.

"Good," Lilli said. "You shouldn't go talk to someone you don't know by yourself, and I think you need more muscle than just you and me to go talk to that Gregory guy. Where does he live anyway? Do you even know?"

"Yep, I saw his name in Stella's address book."

"OK. Then I'm going to go take a shower. I'm still pretty full from lunch. I'll join you in cheesecake and wine after I get into my pjs." She looked at me sitting on the couch. "Are you sure you don't want to share the bed? We could pretend it's a sleepover, like we're kids again. It'll be fun."

I smiled. I knew she was trying to cheer me up.

"Maybe next time. I'll stick to the couch tonight." It would be easier to sneak out in the morning that way.

"Alright. See you in a little bit, De."

I held my glass up in silent agreement as she left the room.

LILLI AMBUSHED ME IN the morning. I got up, sneaked into the bathroom, and was dressed and just about to grab my keys and go when I heard her call my name, from the kitchen.

I walked in. Lilli was adding frothed milk to her coffee. Garren was sitting at the table.

"Busted," he said, pointing his cup of coffee at me.

I narrowed my eyes at him, then looked at Lilli.

"Are you going somewhere, Deana?" she asked innocently. "You haven't had your coffee yet."

I leaned against the wall and crossed my arms.

"Don't worry, it's perking right now. Sit down."

I closed my eyes, let out a long, suffering sigh, and then plopped into a seat.

"She asked for my number last night after you left with Drew," Garren said as he sipped his coffee.

"Did she?"

"Yes, I did. You see, I'm that irritating BFF that's always going to insert herself in your business, whether you like it or not."

She put two teaspoons of sugar in my coffee, stirred it, then added what was left of the frothed milk. She set the mug in front of me.

I wrapped my hands around it, took a sip and then sighed in caffeine-induced pleasure. "You're forgiven for now," I grumbled.

"I sent Garren a text before my shower telling him to get over here early because you had a new lead."

I set the coffee cup down. "Garren, I don't mind if you come along, but I..."

"Great!" Lilli cut in. "You two can go talk to Mr. Martin. I'll stay here and hold down the fort."

The oven timer went off. Lilli opened it and took out a freshly made quiche.

"How long have you been up?" I asked.

"A few hours. You're not the only one who can sneak around, De. Now eat and then go find your rabbit."

"We're doing this my way this time," I said. We were driving to Gregory Martin's in Garren's truck.

"What do you mean?"

"I mean I'll do the talking. I don't want a repeat of what happened at Fuhsaz's with Gus."

"Nothing happened with Gus."

"You went in there and copped an attitude with him."

"He was rude."

"I don't care. You were there for me, for information that we needed to find Stella's rabbit. You weren't there to continue whatever small town drama you have." I turned towards him as he drove. "What if you don't like Gregory Martin? Are you going to talk to him with that same attitude? Because it didn't help with Gus, and it won't help here."

Garren's grip tightened on the wheel. I could see the vein in his temple ticking.

"Fine," he said through clenched teeth. "But for the record, I don't have a problem with Gregory Martin."

"Good," I said.

We pulled up outside Gregory Martin's house.

I rang the doorbell. A man opened the door. He was tall, with a slight stoop to his shoulders. His hair was thick and gray with a little bit of faded brown shot through it. He looked at me and Garren but didn't say anything.

Garren looked over at me. He was taking my request to heart and not saying a word.

"Um, Hi, Mr. Martin? I'm Deana Weber. This is Garren Hewett."

"I know Mr. Hewett," he said. He stepped back from the door and started walking back into his house.

"Don't just stand there. Come on in. I suppose you're here for the rabbit."

My expression had to have matched Garren's wide startled eyes. We stepped inside and shut the door, then followed Gregory. He led us through the house and out a back door, then across the yard to an old barn. We walked inside. I took a moment while my eyes adjusted to the dimmer light inside the building then continued to follow Mr. Martin. He pulled open a barn door halfway through, and there, in a square pen about six feet wide, was Mudd.

CHAPTER FIFTEEN

FOR A STOLEN RABBIT that Garren had suggested was being served up as a main course, Mudd looked particularly well. He looked especially happy as he followed another rabbit around in the pen.

"Is that a girl rabbit?" I asked after watching Mudd attempt the proverbial position.

"Yep," Gregory Martin said, "that's a doe. She's a steel angora. She's a beauty, isn't she?"

And for a man who had been described to me by Garren as a bit gruff, Gregory Martin appeared very happy.

"What is going on?" I quietly asked Garren as we stood watching the rabbits in the pen.

"May I?" Garren asked me as he held his hand out towards Mr. Martin.

"Fine," I said, "just be nice, please."

"Mr. Martin," Garren began.

"I know, I know," Mr. Martin broke in, "I'll get him out. I just wanted you to see that he was alright."

"Mr. Martin," Garren repeated, "have you been breeding Mudd and this doe?"

"Well now, Garren, that is the general idea." He chuckled and stepped into the pen and scooped up Mudd. There was a small travel crate outside of the pen that he set him down in.

"Here you go. I'd give the little guy some extra food for a few days. He has definitely earned it." He chuckled again at the innuendo.

He handed Garren the crate with Mudd. I gave Garren a very confused look, but he shook his head and pushed me towards the door. Mr. Martin led us from the barn to a side gate next to the house. He waved goodbye, still looking very pleased with himself. We were almost at the car when I finally exploded.

"What the heck was that?" I said, reigning my temper in just enough to not yell.

"Put Mudd in the truck and turn it on with the air conditioning set low," he said calmly.

"Why?"

"Because angora rabbits are very prone to heat stroke, and it's a warm, sunny spring day."

"Oh, OK." I turned the truck on and set the air to low, then stood back up.

"Now what?"

"Now I'm going to go back to talk to Mr. Martin and you're going to call the police."

"And say what," I asked slowly, "that he stole a rabbit and just now very happily returned it to us?"

"Yes, he returned Mudd, but only after he used him as a stud to possibly get that doe pregnant. The police will have to confiscate the doe until we, actually until *you* decide if you're going to press charges or take possession of the doe."

"Oh," I said. "But I don't want another rabbit," I whined. "Just call the police. Let's deal with one problem at a time."

He walked back to the house, and I called the police.

It wasn't pretty.

"SO, WHAT HAPPENED?" Lilli asked excitedly.

She had come out to the rabbitry when she saw us pull up and walk through the yard. Garren had the crate. He handed me his keys since I had left my copy in the house. I unlocked the door and held it open for him, then shut it again and stood outside with Lilli.

"He gave us the rabbit back."

"I can see that. Was it difficult? Did he give you guys any trouble?"

"Not at first." I grimaced. "It turns out he stole Mudd so he could try breeding him with another rabbit."

"That's-that's so weird," she said.

"Agreed. But he was really nice about it when we got there: he us in the house, took us back to his barn where he had them, loaded Mudd up in the crate and handed him over. He was very cheerful."

"He *was* cheerful?"

"Yep, until Garren went back and told him he'd have to turn over the doe also. Then it got ugly."

"Ohh." Her eyes went wide, and she crossed her arms, hugging herself. Oddly, she looked even more interested now.

"Lilli, are you happy that there was drama?" I asked her.

"What? Of course not. Well, maybe a little. Come on, De, this is like, CSI with country quaintness." She waved her hand at me. "What happened next?"

I smiled at her excitement. I couldn't help it.

"He, Gregory Martin, started yelling at Garren. Garren had told me to call the police and left me at the truck with Mudd. So, while he and Mr. Martin were arguing the police showed up."

"Was it Andrew?"

"Andrew?" I asked her.

"Officer Turner. You know who I mean."

"Mm-hm," I said. I had the feeling Lilli was enjoying Drew's flirting. "No, it was another officer. He got the basic story from me, then went over to talk with Garren and Mr. Martin. There was more shouting, and then the officer cuffed Mr. Martin. He didn't look very happy anymore."

"So, you've got the rabbit back. It was with the man whom your aunt said it might be with. But you don't look happy."

"Of course I'm not happy. That man stole something from Stella and acted like it was no big deal. And now there's another rabbit, and she might be pregnant, and..."

"Wait, already? He's only been missing a few days."

"You do know how biology works, right? And there is that old saying about sex and rabbits."

She laughed. "That's true. Do you think there will be baby bunnies?"

"Kits." Garren said as he opened the door of the rabbitry and joined us. "They're called kits."

"Aw, how cute." Lilli said.

Garren and I were quiet.

"What am I missing?" Lilli asked.

I waved towards the car.

"Garren has the doe. He's going to take her to the veterinary clinic while we wait to see if she's pregnant."

"And if she is?" Lilli asked.

"If she is then Deana has some choices to make," Garren said.

I threw my hands up in the air and stomped into the house, leaving Lilli and Garren standing there.

CHAPTER SIXTEEN

I SLAMMED THE DOOR behind me as I went into the house. Then I stopped, suddenly feeling completely drained. Lilli found me standing in the middle of the kitchen, shoulders slumped, head in my hands.

"I can't deal with this. I just can't deal with this."

"Deana," Lilli said softly.

"This is just too much, Lilli!" I threw my arms out. "There's a shed full of rabbits out there! I've been questioned about a murder! And now this! I don't want rabbit babies!"

"Kits, hon," she said helpfully. "They're called kits."

I narrowed my eyes at her. "I know what they're called," I said as I clinched my jaw, "and I don't want them."

'Well, there may not be a 'them', so let's just shelve that for now."

She put her arm around me and walked me into the living room.

"I'm gonna get us something to drink," she said. I slumped down onto the couch as she disappeared back into the kitchen and came back with two mugs of hot chocolate.

"What, no wine?"

"It's barely lunch time. Besides, chocolate is just as therapeutic. It's a spiced mocha. Try it, it's pretty good."

"Chocolate and wine could be therapeutic," I suggested.

"I think a clear head would help you most right now."

I sighed heavily and leaned my head back on the couch cushion, then looked over at Lilli. I sat back up and took a sip.

She looked anxiously at me. "Better?"

"Yes, thanks, Lil."

She let out a sigh and relaxed, then took a sip and said, "Therapy would be so much easier if I could serve drinks."

I snorted and took another sip. "What exactly is the spice in this mocha?"

She smiled. "Cinnamon and brandy."

"Ah. That explains it," I murmured as a warm feeling flushed through my system. "What am I going to do?" I sighed.

"It's a lot to deal with," She admitted.

"Yes." I took another sip, then set my glass on the coffee table.

"I'm so mad," I said. She nodded.

"The officer asked if I wanted to press charges. Of course I want to press charges!"

"Did you?"

"Yes. They took Gregory Martin away in the police car. They're going to hold him until tomorrow when the judge will be back."

"Do you know why he took Mudd?" Lilli asked.

"Does it matter?"

"I don't know, De. It just seems like an odd thing to do, unless he had a reason, besides the breeding part obviously."

"Well, I don't care what the reason was," I said as I crossed my arms and leaned back into the couch cushions again.

"Don't you think you should know? I mean, you are having this man arrested."

"Yes, because he stole something. Why are you making me feel like *I'm* doing the wrong thing?"

"Deana, you know I love you and that I think you're a great person. It's just that sometimes you can rush to judgment a little quickly."

"Excuse me?"

"Remember our neighbor, Mrs. James? You thought she was a rude, old woman, who ignored you every time you tried to wave hello to her."

"That's completely different."

"Really? Because it took three months and you walking a package over that had come to us by mistake before you figured out that she was too blind to see you waving."

"How was I supposed to know that?"

"That's not the point. The point is that you jumped to an assumption without knowing everything. Maybe she really was rude, but you never tried to approach her directly to find out. You just made a judgment on how things appeared to you."

"Why are you picking on me?" I whined.

"I'm not," she said laughing. 'Hon, we all have flaws. What kind of friend would I be if I didn't point yours out once in a while?"

"If you were really a friend you'd add more brandy to my mocha," I said, sniffing a little for effect.

She raised her eyes at me. "You're so full of it. But I will take pity on you," she said as she got up and took my mug into the kitchen to top it off. "After all, she called back as she walked away, "you're going to be a mommy soon."

"Ugh!" I groaned as I threw a pillow at her, then flopped back down on the couch and buried my head in the cushions.

LILLI HAD LEFT TO GO back to Philly not long after that. She gave me a hug and told me to give it more thought before I threw the book at the bunny thief, Mr. Martin.

I took a shower, ate some left-over potato salad, and then sat around listening to Aunt Stella's records. Her music preferences fit my mood perfectly. I sat listening to women like Ella Fitzgerald and Bessie Smith sing about pain and suffering and men like John Lee Hooker sing about hard times. I know my present joblessness was temporary and not a daily struggle but add the rabbit drama and the murder questioning and I could relate a little. Is this why Stella was drawn to the music? Did she think of her daily life as a constant struggle because of her health? Somehow, I couldn't picture her wallowing the way that I was doing. And I noticed something else. The male and female singers were both talented and drew out emotional responses, but the men sounded more resigned to their struggle.

The women though, even while singing so deeply of their despair, sounded more defiant to me; giving voice to their pains, but demanding that they would only accept what life gave them on their terms, and would deal with it how they chose.

I went to bed and dreamed about blue rabbits hopping through the house. Every time I opened a door or cabinet more would tumble out, like that tribble episode of *Star Trek*. Diana Ross as Billie Holiday and Frank Sinatra were standing in the living room, on a small stage lit with blue lights. A disco ball hung from the ceiling, reflecting the colored light like a thousand stars. They sang a duet while a man played an electric guitar. I couldn't hear their words over the drawn-out chords of the instrument, only see their expressions as they sang with their eyes closed, their hands clinched around the microphones. Gus Davies sat at a table, humming along to the music as he carved a roasted pig with an apple stuck in its mouth.

I didn't sleep well.

CHAPTER SEVENTEEN

I DROVE TO TOWN HALL early the next morning to find out when Gregory Martin would be brought before the judge. He was scheduled with a few others for ten.

I was sitting outside on a bench, scrolling through my phone while I waited, when a woman spoke to me.

"Hello," she said as she sat down next to me on the bench.

I looked up. She met my eyes and smiled, not overly friendly, just politely enough to expect a reaction.

I gave a small nod back. "Hi."

"You're Deana Weber?"

"Um, yes."

"I'm Mina Rourke. Julie, the receptionist in Town Hall, mentioned you were here."

"Oh, has court started? I thought it was later." I started to get up.

She put a hand on my arm.

"No, you're fine. I'd just like to talk with you. I'm the administrator for Central Region Libraries and I had to be here today for a meeting. I happened to hear that Gregory Martin was arrested."

"Yes," I said. I still had no idea why this woman was talking to me. She was older and dressed very smartly in a plum pants suit. Her black and silver hair was pulled back in a loose twist, showing the small gold earrings dangling from her ears. The only other jewelry was a two-toned watch on her wrist and a plain band on her ring finger.

"And you're pressing charges against him for stealing a rabbit?"

"I know, it sounds silly, but..."

"But stealing is a crime," she finished. She looked at me for a moment then said, "You work for PLC. Do you enjoy it?"

"I *worked* for them," I said, correcting her, "and yes, I did enjoy it. How do you know that?"

"Your aunt told me."

I was still confused. She sat back on the bench, no longer looking at me.

"I've known Stella Woods a long time. We're both from Chicago, though a few years apart. I kicked her out of the blues club where I was waiting tables. She was underage then," she looked over at me and smiled.

"I bet it's hard for you to think of your aunt as a young girl."

"Um, I guess. Yes," I admitted, thinking of Stella's eclectic music collection.

"Mm-hmm. Well, don't worry, you'll sit where I am one day. If you're lucky."

I stayed silent, still not sure why she was talking to me.

"Does Stella still have my 'Smoke Stack Lightning'?" she asked.

"Maybe? I don't know what that is." It seemed odd to me that she was still referring to Stella in the present tense, and I realized that she might not know that Aunt Stella had died. "I don't know if you know," I said slowly, not wanting to shock the woman, "but Stella died."

"Oh, I know," she said. "I missed the service in the village. I knew about her heart condition, though. So, whenever we caught up with each other we made sure to leave nothing unsaid. I knew your aunt very well, you see." She turned to me.

"I also know why Gregory Martin did what he did. My question is, do you?"

I heard Lilli in my head asking me almost the same thing.

"I don't," I said.

"Would you like to know?"

I sighed. "I have a feeling I need to know."

"Good girl," she said. "Stella always said you were smart, just a little rigid."

I pursed my mouth in a frown.

She chuckled. "She knew you well. Now, let me tell you about the Stella I knew."

I was still frowning but sat back and listened.

"I don't think Stella ever wanted to be tied down, not in the traditional sense. She never wanted marriage, hardly ever dated for more than a few months. That girl just could not commit to the long term — it doesn't mean she never found love though.

She fell in love a few times. Still, she wouldn't stay put. Then she found Fox Cove. She lived there the longest she had lived anywhere. I thought she had finally found her place, her home. And she had. She also found love there. Gregory Martin."

My mouth dropped open. "Gregory Martin? You've got to be kidding me. That can't be right. She left a video, Mrs.

Rourke. She said that if something happened to the rabbits to look for Gregory Martin. She didn't sound like she loved the guy even if she dated him for a while."

"Love doesn't always equal happy endings, Deana. She did love him, and he loved her. He loved her so much that after they had been dating for about a year he proposed. He thought they were perfect together, that they could spend the rest of their lives together. But Stella said no.

She broke his heart. Not on purpose, of course. She did love him. Maybe she would have even stayed with him, if not forever than maybe for a few years. That would have been a first for her. But she told me she knew he wouldn't have settled for that. It was all or nothing for him, so she gave him nothing.

He chased after her for a while, but then gave that up too. She told me the last thing he ever said to her was that she had stolen his heart, and one day he would steal hers."

"So, he stole her rabbit after she died? That doesn't really make sense."

"It does if you know where she got the rabbit. Do you?"

"No, but I bet you're going to tell me."

"Gregory Martin gave it to her. Muddy Waters was the first rabbit she ever had. He was a valentine's gift from Gregory. Stella had never had a pet, never had children. She fell in love with that stupid rabbit, and Gregory knew it."

"So, he knew if he stole Mudd that he would be stealing Stella's heart," I said. I finally understood why a grown man would do such a stupid thing. And I began to wonder if having him arrested was a stupid thing for me to do.

Mina Rourke gave me a serious look.

"What will you do now that you know, Deana?"

I sighed. "It's still wrong, what he did."

"True."

We sat in silence for a moment. The bench sat across the street from Town Hall, close to an intersection. We watched traffic move by us; people walked by chatting. I heard birds chirping in the trees that shaded our seat, singing happily above the noise of the town below.

"What if there were another way to deal with this?" she asked.

"Like what?"

"Before courts were so easily available, communities had to handle local problems themselves. What if the village could mediate?"

"How would they do that?"

"That's details," she said, dismissively waving her hand. "If they could mediate, would you be willing to allow them to decide what happens with Gregory? It wouldn't involve jail. It would be more of an honor system, but I think I understand Gregory Martin enough through Stella to believe he would honor whatever decision they made."

I chewed on my lip as I thought about what she was suggesting. As odd as it sounded, I was more open to her idea than to going after Mr. Martin in court.

"I'm willing to try if he is."

"Good, I'll go talk to him. Come in with me. If he agrees, you can drop the charges here. Then I'll make some calls."

I followed her back into the building and sat in the lobby. Julie, the receptionist looked up and smiled at me, then went back to whatever she was doing. Less than twenty minutes later — I know because I kept looking at the time on my cell — Mrs.

Rourke came back out to tell me that Mr. Martin had agreed to her idea. She had already been on the phone with someone in Fox Cove as well, and we would all meet there tomorrow. I went through the process of dropping the charges against Gregory Martin, not that he thanked me, and then left.

SINCE IT WAS NOW CLOSE to lunchtime and my stomach was growling very loudly to remind me of that fact, I got back to Fox Cove and drove towards the Sparrow. I could already imagine how good the egg salad sandwich would be. I was passing the entrance to Village Park when a blue car pulled out right in front of me. I had to slam on my brakes to avoid running into it.

"Dammit!" I shouted. I saw the car driving away in my rear-view mirror, noticing the same lime green sticker on the back window that I had seen on the Tesla parked outside of the cafe last Tuesday.

"What is the point of buying an expensive hybrid car if you're still going to drive like an imbecile?" I yelled at the retreating car. I tried to shake off the adrenaline and started driving again. I parked and walked into the Sparrow.

It was busy as usual. Trinity Loughlin was behind the register. As I walked up to order she gave me a friendly nod. That was a surprise, considering she had barely spoken to me before.

"Ms. Weber, what can I get you?"

"The egg salad sandwich, please, and an iced tea."

She rang up my order. I paid and was stepping over to wait when she said, "It's a good thing you're doing. Your aunt would approve."

She didn't wait for me to answer, just started helping the next person in line. Having no idea what she meant — it seemed to be a theme for me today — I stood and waited for my food.

I had taken the last wonderful bite of my sandwich and was drinking my tea when Gwen ran in. She looked around, saw me and rushed over.

"I thought I recognized your car outside. I'm so glad I caught you. Now, if it's OK with you we're going to meet this evening after work, say around six? Nan Carson can't make it tomorrow and that would leave us short the necessary number." She stopped talking and took a breath, finally. She smiled expectantly at me.

"Um, Gwen, what are you talking about?"

"The mediation, silly. You talked with Mina Rourke earlier? Well, she called Emory, and he sent out the email letting us know."

"Letting who know, and about what?"

"The ViVos, the Village Volunteer committee. We're going to mediate your problem with Gregory Martin! Except for Eric Tresser, of course, because he's Gregory's oldest friend, so we called in Nan as a sub, but she's only available today. So, are you OK with today?"

I rubbed my hands over my face, then looked back up at her.

"Sure, I guess today is fine."

"Great! I'll let everyone know. I'm so excited. This is the first mediation I've done. The last one was ten years ago when Karl Miller's son drove his car through the village green, right out there. He almost hit the church. The kid was drunk as a skunk. I was out of town for a fabric festival in Sante Fe, so I missed it."

"That's a shame," I said. My sarcasm was lost on her.

"I know, but I'm here now. We're going to meet in the old dance hall, across from Fuhsaz's Antiques. Did you hear what happened there? The owner, Augustus Davies, was found dead."

She paused and said in a mock whisper, "I've heard it might not be an accident. Can you believe it, murder in this little place? I just can't even imagine it."

She obviously hadn't heard that I was on the list of possible suspects, which I was grateful for.

"That's terrible," I said.

"We'll talk about it later," she said, dismissing a death and possible murder as just another piece of news. "I've got to get back to the store. I'll see you at six. Don't be late," she called as she rushed back out.

CHAPTER EIGHTEEN

I WAS BACK IN THE VILLAGE at 6 PM, standing in front of a large wood frame building that Gwen had directed me to. There was a set of very large barn doors with a smaller standard sized door off to the side. I walked inside and stood at the back of the room. Gwen was standing at the front of the room, Emory and Trinity beside her. Two more men and women were in their group. Another man stood at a podium. Gwen saw me and headed my way.

"Hi, Deana. We're all here, just waiting for Eric to call the meeting to order. He's the man at the podium."

Just then Eric rapped the podium with his gavel. Gwen told me to sit at the back. I sat down. There was a noise and I looked to my right. A few yards away Gregory Martin was sitting in a chair by himself. It appeared we would both be spectators at the mediation.

Eric introduced himself, made everyone aware that the meeting was being recorded and then started the mediation. It took about forty-five minutes. Gregory and I sat in the back listening to the events. Stella's relationship with him was mentioned briefly, and their break-up. I had the feeling that no one really knew how badly it had hurt Gregory, except maybe

Eric Tresser. For a moment I saw him look over at his friend. He looked sympathetic, but not like it was a complete surprise. I looked over at Gregory then. His head hung low. He looked like a man who had already given up.

In the end the decision was five to two, though all sides were in my favor. The two who disagreed thought that I should take possession of any kits resulting from breeding the rabbits, but also thought that Gregory should have to give up his doe. I was thankful the other five had the majority decision which allowed Gregory to keep his rabbit. The last thing I needed was *another* rabbit, though if there were babies I'd have that problem anyway.

Eric Tresser gave Gregory and I the official decision and asked if we accepted it. I nodded, but he told me to voice my assent for the recording. I did, and then Gregory agreed as well. He left right after that, not speaking to anyone else.

I stepped outside, feeling completely worn out.

Gwen and Emory followed me out and made sure I was doing alright.

"That was difficult," Emory said as he patted me on my shoulder.

"Yes," Gwen nodded, "but I think it was fair. Do you think so, Deana?"

"I do," I said. "Though I still feel bad for Gregory Martin."

"That means you're a good person," Emory said as he patted my shoulder again.

"Not really. My first reaction was to lock him away in jail."

"We work with the systems we have," Gwen said. "I'm just glad our village had another option."

"Me too," I said, "I think I...do you guys see that?" I asked.

"What?" Gwen asked.

I motioned towards the antiques shop across the street.

"I saw a light moving inside Fuhsaz's."

"It should be closed," Emory said. "Augustus ran it by himself. I believe the police are reaching out to his next of kin, but until they've contacted someone there shouldn't be anyone in there."

I looked up and down the street. I noticed the blue end of a car behind an older pickup truck. From what I could see it looked exactly like the same car that I had seen before.

"Do you guys know anyone in town with a blue Tesla?" I asked.

They both shook their heads.

"Then why have I seen that car multiple times in the past week? Oh, there it is again! The light, do you see it?"

They looked at the store in the darkening light. Clouds were collecting across the valley and rolling towards the village, hastening the coming sunset.

"I see it!" Emory whispered.

"Why are you whispering?" Gwen asked as she whispered back.

He looked at her, realized what he had done and frowned. "Why are you?"

"Because you were. Ugh," she groaned. "What should we do?"

"I think we should call the police," I whispered.

"Now she's doing it," Emory said.

I crossed the road, ignoring them, my cell phone held tight in my hand. I ducked behind a car parked between me and the store, then dialed 911. I told the dispatcher where I was and that there was a suspicious light coming from the store where a murder had been committed recently. When he asked my name he said, "Is this the same Deana Weber that called in a bear last week? You know, making false emergency calls is a waste of department resources, Ms. Weber."

"This is not a false emergency, and neither was that," I argued. "And anyway, I have two other witnesses this time."

He said he was sending an officer and to remain at a safe distance.

I hung up.

"What did they say?" a voice whispered from behind me.

I jumped and almost fell on my backside. "Why are you sneaking up on me, Gwen? You scared me half to death!"

"Shh, Deana. Don't talk so loud."

"Look, look!" I said, trying to whisper as I felt my adrenalin spike. There was a shadow moving along the side of the building. I could just see the form of a person rushing around to the front in the dimming light.

"We have to stop them," I said. "The police aren't here yet."

"What are we supposed to do?"

I chewed on my lip, trying to think of something. Suddenly I grabbed her arm.

"Do you have Emory's cell number?"

"Of course," she said.

"Text him. See if he can block that blue car down the street. I think it belongs to the person who murdered Gus. We can't let it leave."

Gwen texted Emory as we huddled behind the parked car. We saw him look at his phone from where he was standing near the old dance hall. He ran back inside and came out a moment later with Eric Tresser. Eric walked over and opened the door to the truck parked next to the blue car. He got in and started it, backed it out, and then stopped in the street, effectively blocking the car parked beside him. The engine shut off and we saw him get out. He walked around to the front and lifted the hood, then just stood there.

Gwen and I stood up and tried to appear like we were just walking by as we crossed the street and met back up with Emory.

"What's he doing?" Gwen asked.

"I told him that there was a possible robbery and that I wanted him to block a car in with his truck to stop the person from driving away," Emory said. "He said sure and came right out."

"Seriously?" I asked. "He didn't think that was strange?"

Emory shrugged. "Eric's very good in emergency situations. It's why he's the head of our phone tree."

"He was a medic in the military," Gwen said.

We watched as the person we had seen, first shining a flashlight around the store and then sneaking out of it, ran towards his car, which was now blocked in by Eric's truck.

"Hey, move your truck, man!" the guy shouted at Eric. He was tall and skinny, wearing a denim shirt over a t-shirt. He was wearing a baseball cap so I couldn't see his features very well, but he sounded like he was from the city. The three of us walked a little closer, pulled in as much by curiosity as by the knowledge that this guy might be a robber, or worse, a murderer.

"Sorry," Eric was saying to him. "It just stalled. I can't get the engine to turn over."

The guy started arguing with Eric, and Eric kept apologizing, acting like he couldn't figure out what to do with the truck. The guy went to his car, opened the door and threw something in, then turned and started shouting at Eric again.

I finally saw the police car pull around the corner of the street. Officer Andrew Turner was driving. He parked his car in the street behind Eric's truck and stepped out of his cruiser.

"What's the problem?" he asked.

"Not sure," Eric said cryptically.

"I just want to get my car out," the guy in the cap said. He looked a little nervous now.

"And you are?" Drew asked very seriously.

"No one, man," the guy said.

"What's that?" Drew asked him as he pointed towards the guy's pants.

"No-nothing, just a flashlight."

"You usually walk around with a flashlight in your back pocket, Mr.—?"

"Baker. My name is Paul Baker. I just needed it to look for something I dropped."

"What did you drop?"

"What? Oh, it's not important. Look, I really need to leave. Could we move this truck, maybe roll it forward?"

"That's not very neighborly of you, Mr. Baker." Drew said as he walked over to Paul Baker's car.

"Nice car," he said. "Tesla. Is this one of those hybrid electric cars? I'm never sure about the electric system. It seems odd." He looked in the car window.

"Would you open your car, Mr. Baker?"

"What? Why? I'm not the one blocking the street, he is," Paul Baker said as he pointed at Eric. Eric spread his hands in a helpless gesture.

"Mr. Baker, I'm going to ask you again to open your car." Drew said.

"Open it yourself, man," Paul Baker said tersely. "I just want to leave."

"OK, thanks," Drew said as he reached for the handle of the car door. He opened the door, reached in and stood back up, holding a work glove by the tip of his pen.

"Is this blood, Mr. Baker?" he asked.

"Those aren't mine, man. I borrowed them."

"Mr. Baker, I'm going to need you to face the car and put your hands on the hood."

Another police car had pulled up while we were watching the exchange between Drew and Paul Baker. The second officer put the now cuffed Mr. Baker in the back of his police car. Drew spoke to Eric Tresser, who started his truck and moved it down a few parking spaces. Then Eric walked over to where I was standing with Gwen and Emory.

"I'm sure I'm going to get a very good explanation for all of this," he said to us.

Gwen began speaking for all of us as she told him what we had seen and then done to get the police here to stop the man, Mr. Baker, from getting away.

"Do you think this guy, Paul Baker, might be the guy who murdered Augustus Davies?" Eric asked us.

"Oh, yes," Gwen said.

"And you think forcing him to stay stuck here, a possible murderer, in the area, was the safest thing to do?"

Well…" Emory said. Gwen looked down sheepishly and shrugged.

"It's my fault," I said. "I over-reacted when I saw the light in the store. The police had questioned me because my prints were on the murder weapon, and I was just hoping that finding the real murderer would clear me."

"What!" Gwen and Emory both shouted.

"Oh, yeah, I forgot to mention that didn't I?"

They both looked at me, still shocked.

"Well," Eric Tresser said, "I'm going home and going to bed. I've got a produce delivery at 3 AM. Goodnight, all."

He walked away, spoke to Drew for a moment and must have been given permission to leave. He backed his truck out and drove down the street.

Drew walked over to our group.

"I'm going to need statements from the three of you before you can go."

"Of course," I said. "Did he do it?"

"Yes, did he?" Gwen asked, wringing her hands. "Did he kill Gus?"

Drew looked back at the police car where Paul Baker sat.

"He's denying that he did anything but accompany the man who murdered Augustus Davies. He also admitted to breaking into the store tonight, but said the other guy was who we wanted. We'll sort it out. But you're in the clear, Ms. Weber. He did corroborate that when he was in there before he set the books between the bookends."

"I'm so glad," I said dryly.

"Deana…" Drew started to say.

"No, it's fine, Officer Turner. You were just doing your job."

"Then why are you calling me Officer Turner?"

"Have you ever been questioned by the police? It's not a comfortable experience."

I waved away whatever he was going to say next.

"Really, it's fine. Right now, I'm tired. It's been a very, very long day. Just let me give my statement so I can go home and get some sleep."

"You're driving back to Philadelphia?" he asked, looking concerned.

"No, just to Stella's house."

"Oh, OK. You said 'home.'"

"Well, home for tonight at least."

We each gave our statements. I said goodnight to Gwen and Emory and drove the short distance to Stella's.

It took me very little time to climb into my pjs and set up the couch. I flipped through Stella's photo album a little bit that I had left on the coffee table. There were a couple of photos that showed a younger Stella with whom I realized was my mom. They were caught in laughter on the green of what looked like a college campus. I smiled at the two young women in the photo, then got a little sad. I had the same thought I had before when listening to Stella's blues music. Did the younger Stella in the photo think all of the time of how short her life could be because of her faulty heart? How does a person go through every day knowing something like that? I set the album aside and laid back on the pillows I had stacked on one end of the couch, pulling the sheet up around me. I was falling asleep as I thought about the randomness of life, how we could make all the plans we wanted, but in the end our plans were still dependent on so many things out of our control.

CHAPTER NINETEEN

AND TO FURTHER COMPLICATE any decisions I needed to make, Mina Rourke called the next day as I was packing up to head back to Philly.

I had woken up, feeling quite good about life. The murder was solved, at least enough that my innocence was no longer in question. The rabbit drama had been concluded and I had decided that my mom should have to make the major decisions about what to do with the house and rabbitry. Stella had been her oldest friend after all. As her only daughter, I was just along for the ride as the next female in line.

In the kitchen I had decided to tackle the espresso maker and had made a somewhat drinkable cup of coffee. By my second cup I felt capable enough that I made an extra cup and then walked with it out to the rabbitry. It was still early, and I had seen Garren walk through the garden while I sat at the kitchen table. He waved when he saw me and then had gone into the building.

I walked out with the espresso and knocked, then eased the door open a little.

"May I come in?" I asked.

"It is your place, Deana. You don't have to ask."

I stepped all the way in and shut the door behind me.

"Good morning," he said.

"Good morning. I made you an espresso," I said as I held out the small cup. "You don't have to drink it if you don't want. It's only the third cup I've made on that machine so it may not be that good." *Why was I babbling so much?*

He smiled. "I'd love it. Thanks." He set aside the scoop he was using to pour pellets for the rabbits' food and took the cup from me. He took a sip. His eyes got a little large but then he took another sip. "It's not bad. A little strong. Do you want to know a secret?"

"Um, sure."

"Try a little salt next time, in with the grounds. The coffee is affected a lot by the water that it's made with, and Stella's water is a little hard. The salt will temper the bitterness just a little bit."

"Oh. Okay. How do you know that?"

He smiled. "My father is a chef who's worked in many countries. It's something you learn in the food industry."

"Oh." I smiled back. "Can I help with anything here?"

"Of course. Why don't you start adding hay to all their bins. Pack it in a little so they don't run out. They'll eat it all day if they have it. I've already finished cleaning their droppings from the pullout trays. I've been taking it to my parents' garden for fertilizer. Rabbit manure is very good for gardens. Is it alright if I keep doing that? Stella said she always had more than enough to share, but you could also be selling it, so it's up to you."

I made a face. "No. You can take the very useful rabbit poop. Enjoy it with my blessing. Besides, I still have to talk with my mom about all of this, so it'll be a while before we figure out what to do. You'll have to let me know when you're paid time is up also so we can work out a new schedule, if you can still help of course."

"I can. Don't worry about these guys."

"I'm going to miss them a little bit."

Garren laughed. "I thought they made you nuts."

"It's just a lot of responsibility." I walked over to Bessie's hutch. She was happily chewing on the hay in her bin. I opened her door just enough to reach in and run my hand over her fur. She moved away a little but then came back and pulled more hay to nibble on. I continued to smooth the fur over her back. A few strands came away in my hand. I rolled them between my fingers as I shut the door.

"I guess they've grown on me. I didn't realize they could be so playful and cuddly."

"They can be mean too. Don't let their cuddliness fool you."

I smiled, shuffling my feet as I stood there suddenly feeling awkward. I watched him take another sip of espresso, watched his arm move slightly, making the muscles under his shirt flex. "I guess I should get back inside and keep packing. I'll take the cup if you're done."

He tipped the demitasse cup back and finished the last bit of coffee, then handed it to me.

"Do you think you'll come back here?" he asked.

"Probably. I'm sure I'll need to help pack things up at some point."

"Would you let me know if you come back? I mean, I'd like to be here to see you again, if that's alright."

"Um, sure. I'll let you know."

Our eyes met briefly before I turned away to leave.

Was that interest I saw in his eyes as he looked back at me?

I was still contemplating the possibility that Garren was interested in me when I went back inside the house. I only had a few things to pack so it didn't take long for me to be ready to go. I felt a little sad. I was happy to be heading back to Philadelphia. I had a life to get back to and figure out. But I also realized I would miss the people I had met here, even miss those silly rabbits a little bit. I went over to Stella's music collection and pulled out a record. It seemed fitting that it ended up being a cover featuring Muddy Waters. On a whim I decided to take it with me. I slid it into the canvas grocery bag, between the two photo albums I had also packed to take back with me. I carried it and walked over to pick up my overnight bag so I could start loading my car. My phone rang just as I reached down for the bag; another Pennsylvania number that I didn't recognize.

"Hello?" I said.

"Hello, Deana? This is Mina Rourke. I hope you don't mind. I got your number from George Lewis at the PLC."

"My old boss? No, that's fine, but why?"

"I inquired about you after we spoke the other day. I had a feeling, and I've learned to listen to my gut when it tells me something. George had some very nice things to say about you."

"Mr. Lewis is a good man. I enjoyed working for him, but I'm not working there anymore."

'Yes, I'm aware that you were laid off due to the budget cuts and mergers. It's a shame when these things happen, but in our business it's not really a surprise either." She paused and I thought the call was wrapping up, but she started speaking again a moment later. "Honestly, I think your bad luck at being laid off may be just what I need."

"Um...I don't understand."

"I told you before I'm the library administrator for Central Region. I've been working on a program with Cumberland County. We have a generous benefactor that enjoys spreading literature as far as she can. Thanks to her, I now have three mobile truck units and a volunteer crew of builders and carpenters that have outfitted them for use as mobile libraries. I believe they even have a couple of on-board computer stations. Our county had economic difficulties a few years ago as well. We had to reduce some of our physical locations. However, it occurred to me that the brick-and-mortar buildings we lost could be replaced in part by more economical options. Because of this generous donation, I've been able to test my idea."

"That sounds interesting," I said.

"I can't take full credit for the idea. Many countries with limited resources use these types of libraries to share their resources. Plus, I love watching those tiny house shows on TV. Could you imagine one of those tiny spaces as a miniature library?"

I smiled, silently agreeing with her. I was still confused though. *Why was she calling me?*

"I still don't understand what this has to do with me, Mrs. Rourke."

"It just didn't sit well with me that our rural communities were suddenly cut off from our services unless they traveled longer distances. We're here to serve them after all."

"I agree. But..."

"I'm getting there, Deana. Just be patient."

I sighed. I set my stuff back down and walked over to the couch, sinking onto it as I tried to wait for her to get to the reason she had called.

I heard her laugh through my phone. "Oh, to be young again. So impatient to go, go, go," she mused. "I'm glad you have some spunk."

"Thanks," I said dryly.

She ignored my tone and continued. "When I spoke to you in Pekan Township I was there for a meeting."

"Yes, you mentioned that."

"The meeting was to decide on the beta locations for the three mobile units. For this program to succeed and move forward I need to place the units in areas where I can be fairly certain they will be utilized. Fox Cove had been one of those areas until the librarian who lived near there retired and moved south."

"That's too bad."

"It is, yes, or was. You see, if *you* were living in Fox Cove then it would make it a viable option again."

"But I live in Philadelphia."

"I realize that. However, I also know that Stella has left you and your mother her estate, which includes a nice little home in Fox Cove."

I could feel a tension headache building over my eyes. I rubbed my forehead, trying to smooth away the stress I felt growing.

"How do you know that?"

"Deana, I'm a librarian. I know many things." She chuckled. "Also, Stella used me as a witness when she made her will. She shared her intentions with me then. I told you; Stella Woods and I go way back."

"Oh. Well, I haven't even spoken with my mom yet about the estate. I really have no idea what's going to happen with it. But — are you offering me a job, Mrs. Rourke?"

"Yes, Deana. I'd like you to run the mobile library in Fox Cove. It would only be three days a week. The other two days you would work out of the branch in Pekan Township, alongside other staff, but the management of the mobile library would fall to you, with oversight by me of course. George assured me that you are more than ready to take on a management role, a sentiment that only reinforced my own opinion after meeting with you. What you did for Gregory Martin was a difficult decision, but it showed that you had the ability to make tough choices that still put the community first. So, I'd like to officially offer you a semi-managerial position with the Central Region libraries. What do say?"

"I-I'm not sure. I'm very flattered by the offer. But it's a huge surprise." I leaned back, too shocked to think straight.

"May I think about it? I'm driving back to Philadelphia today, right now actually."

"Of course! Only, I'll need an answer soon, by the end of the week unfortunately."

"Oh, okay. I do appreciate the offer. It's a wonderful opportunity. How much does it pay, by the way?"

"Ah, so you are budget conscious as well. That's good. How about you call me once you're back in the city and I'll give you more details about the position. Would that work for you?"

"Yes, thank you. I'll call tomorrow. I promise."

"I'll hold you to it. Have a safe drive back."

I hung up with Mrs. Rourke and breathed a huge sigh.

Once again, I grabbed my stuff and loaded it in my car. I walked back in the house to check it once more before I locked up. As I was looking around the living room, I noticed the DVD case still sitting by the TV. I had left Stella's video in the machine and forgotten about it. I turned the system back on to remove it but must have hit the play button by mistake. Instead of restarting at the beginning of the recording the video resumed from where it had stopped playing before. The blank screen came on and I was about to stop and eject it when the screen changed, and Stella's image appeared again. She started speaking.

"Sorry about that. I just needed a moment. Where was I? Oh, yes, Gregory. As I was saying, Gregory and I were together, and it was good between us. But he wanted more from me. He wanted to get married, live together, build a life together. I just couldn't do it, Celia. I've been on my own too long. As much as I loved the man, I couldn't give him the commitment he wanted from me. I also hadn't told him my whole medical history. I know I should have, and I did give him a vague explanation about having a chronic condition, but I'm sure he assumed it was something common, and I let him. I don't know why. I guess it was just easier for me that way."

Stella's image looked out her kitchen window. She brought her hand to her face, covering her mouth for a moment with her fingers. I could see her hand shaking a little as she patted her face, then wiped at her eyes. She looked back and then down and said quietly, "Maybe I should have tried things his way. Maybe I should have opened up to him completely. It's not easy to change old habits.

But if I'm gone now, if I've died, then Gregory will be hurting, and I don't want that. I did love him, still do if I'm honest, and even if it's too late for me to go back and fix what I did I'd still like to make amends. So, talk to Gregory, please. He'll take care of the rabbits if no one else can. He may just take Mudd, and that's alright, but he can also help to find them all good homes. He gave me that silly rabbit after all, started this whole funny hobby for me.

Celia, I know you and Robert have a great marriage. Keep doing that, keep being there for each other. And Deana, if you're watching, quit living your life inside those books you love so much. They're wonderful escapes, I know. They got me through many post-op therapies. But life must be lived among people.

I love you all. Give my love to the boys."

The screen went blank again. I let it play awhile this time just to make sure it was the end of the recording. I ejected the disc and put it in the case, then went in the bathroom and washed my face and blew my nose. If only I had watched the stupid video completely before. None of the rabbit drama would have had to happen. I didn't know what to do now.

CHAPTER TWENTY

AFTER WATCHING THE rest of Stella's video, it seemed serendipitous that I saw Gregory Martin when I stopped at the Sparrow Cafe for breakfast. He was sitting on the bench outside with a newspaper, but he had it folded in his lap, not reading it. He still looked pretty despondent about the mediation decision. I felt better that I had gone with the mediation instead of seeing him arrested and charged with a crime, but I still felt like something was unresolved. I thought about Stella's video, how she had gone on to explain about her difficulty with letting love fully into her life, how she had regretted holding back and still causing the suffering that she had tried to avoid. Gregory Martin had been punished for his crime, but the reasons he had done it were still weighing on me.

I suddenly had an idea. I grabbed the album full of photos of Stella's rabbits. The one at the very front, the first photo, showed me all the answers I needed. I hoped it would give Gregory Martin the same closure. I slid the photo into my purse and got out of my car.

"Mr. Martin?" I said as I approached him. "Hi."

He looked up at me. "Ms. Weber. I'm sorry — for the trouble I've caused. It was never my intention. I would've never done anything to hurt Stella, or her rabbits."

"I know," I said. I stood in front of him, looking down at him as he looked down at the ground.

"Would you have coffee with me? There's something I want to show you."

He reluctantly agreed. We went inside the cafe. I ordered my coffee and a lemon poppy muffin. He got his coffee, and we found a table away from the small crowd and sat down.

I really wasn't sure how to start this conversation. It had been a spur of the moment idea, a sudden understanding of two people that I didn't really know. I wanted it to go well, to be what we both needed for closure. *Here goes nothing*, I thought.

But as I took a breath to begin speaking, Gregory also started talking.

"It must seem silly to you, an old fool like me getting so emotional over a rabbit. I never meant to cause any harm," he said as he looked down at the top of the table. "I want you to know that, Ms. Weber." He raised his face and met my eyes. "I just wanted something, a part of Stella, to hold on to. I never stopped loving her, you see."

"I don't think it's silly at all, Mr. Martin. Maybe just not the best way to deal with things, the stealing I mean."

He nodded, grimacing at being reminded of what he had done.

It felt like a good time to do what I had intended to do when I asked him to talk with me. I reached into my purse and took out the photo. I looked at it again and then handed it to him.

"This was in Stella's photo album," I said, "the one she had full of pictures of her rabbits."

He looked down at the photo in his hand. It showed him and Stella standing together. Stella was holding Mudd and Gregory had an arm around her shoulders as he smiled at the camera. They both looked happy.

"She won 'Best in Show' with him that day," he said. "It was her first leg; that's what they call a win like that in rabbit shows. She was so happy."

"She does look happy," I said. "You both do. But Mr. Martin, she's not looking at Mudd or at the camera." I tapped the photo lightly. "She's looking at you. It wasn't the win, or the leg, or Mudd that put that smile on her face. It was having you there with her."

He shook his head. "You can't know that."

"Yes, I can. There may be a lot I didn't know about Aunt Stella, but I know that if she loved you she let you know, and if you were nobody to her she would still be nice, but she wouldn't spend time with you. And the way she's looking at you? I've seen that same look on my dad's face whenever he looks at my mom and she doesn't know he's looking." I twined my hands together and said quietly, "She loved you, Mr. Martin. It may not have been the way you needed or wanted, but it was real."

I saw his shoulders begin to shake. He sat there, crying silently. A few tears dropped onto the picture, and he wiped them away. He took out a handkerchief and smoothed it over the picture again, gently wiping the smudges from it. Then he wiped his eyes, sniffed and gathered himself together.

"May I keep this?" he asked, holding up the photo.

"Of course," I said, "and one more thing. I want you to take Mudd."

He looked at me with surprise and a bit of hope in his expression.

"I can keep him?"

"Yes. I think Stella would like that. In fact, I'm sure of it."

"I'm grateful to you, Ms. Weber."

"Please, call me Deana."

He nodded. "I think that you should keep the doe and the kits. I wouldn't want to separate those babies from their mom. Plus, I'm not very proud of myself for what I did. It's enough that you're letting me have Mudd."

I spoke with Gregory a little longer. Before I left, I told him that I would talk to Garren and let him know what I had decided about Mudd. I left feeling like a weight had been lifted off me.

I SENT LILLI A TEXT before I left the village, letting her know that I was heading back to Philly.

> Leaving Fox Cove now. No longer POI. Details
> when I get there.

My phone buzzed with her response as I was driving through the village. I looked at her text after I pulled up to the four-way stop sign before the turn up to the hill.

Yeah! See U soon.

I stuck my phone in my purse and began to drive away. As I was driving over the little bridge a truck began honking loudly behind me. I looked in my rear view and then in my side mirror, finally making out that it was Garren's truck behind me. I stopped just past the bridge and pulled off the road. *Darn, what now?*

I stepped out of my car and walked back towards where Garren had pulled off on the other side of the bridge.

"What's wrong?" I asked anxiously.

"Nothing," he said as he walked towards me. We met in the center of the bridge.

"Then why were you honking like a maniac? I thought you were going to tell me a bear ate the rabbits, or the shed burned down, or something equally horrible."

"What is it with you and bears?" he asked. He stopped in front of me and smiled. "The rabbits are fine. Everything is fine."

"Oh, okay. So, then why...?" I spread my arm out.

"Why was I honking like a maniac?" he asked, still smiling.

"It was a little maniacal." I said as I smiled back.

He took my hands in his. "I just wanted to make sure that before you left — that I gave you a reason to come back."

"Well, there's the rabbits," I said helpfully, "and the house, and all of the stuff in the house."

"True, but I thought I should give you a more personal reason."

"Personal? What kind of reason would be personal?"

"Um, maybe something like a very personal kiss goodbye," he whispered as he stepped closer to me.

"Ohh," I said breathlessly. "Well, that would be personal."

I felt his warm breath on my lips a second before I felt his mouth touch mine. *He tastes like pepper and honey*, I thought, right before I stopped thinking.

He broke the kiss a moment later, stepping back and giving me a lazy smile. I'm certain that I wore a similar look.

"So, do you think you'll come back?" he asked.

I looked at him, so many thoughts rushing back into my brain that I couldn't focus on any one of them.

"I think," I said, as I stared into his warm brown eyes, "that you've given me a lot to think about."

"Well then, I will let you think, and maybe you'll share those thoughts with me soon."

"Alright."

"Drive safely, Deana Weber and think good thoughts."

"You too," I said lamely.

I spent the drive back to Philly thinking of that delicious kiss, and also about Mina Rourke's offer. It sounded like an interesting project, and the idea that I would manage the mobile unit was enticing. I just wasn't sure about leaving what had been my home for six years. I loved Philadelphia. I loved the city vibe that mixed parks and bike trails with shops and restaurants that were close enough to walk to. I loved all the different concerts and events that were always available. Even its more worn and rough edges had become a familiar part of my life.

There were downsides too, of course. Traffic could be crazy, and sometimes there were less than pleasant smells around the neighborhood. Also, crime was an issue, but that was true of any large city, and between the animal theft and the murder in Fox Cove it was a fact of life that crime could happen anywhere. Still, could I really leave it all for a tiny, little village that barely existed on a map, and didn't even show up on GPS?

Two hours later I still didn't know what to do, not about Garren or the job offer, but I had arrived home. I walked through the front door, set my bags down and went into the kitchen where I heard music and singing. Lilli was 'shaking it off' with Taylor Swift as she listened to her iPod and sliced vegetables.

"Is this what I have to look forward to in my thirties," I said as I walked in, "regression?"

She set the knife down and danced over to me, giving me a hug and making me twirl with her.

"Age is a state of mind," she said, "Don't worry, my young friend, you'll find out soon enough." She twirled back over to the counter.

"So how do you feel now that you're no longer a wanted criminal? And what were you thinking," she said as she swatted at me, "trying to stop a suspected murderer like that?"

I gave her a confused look.

"Drew told me everything," she said.

"Oh, really? Drew, huh? Have you spoken to *Drew* a lot lately?"

"Don't change the subject."

She threw the tomato and cucumber she had sliced on top of mixed greens she had in a bowl. "You could have been hurt, Deana. Did you and your village friends think of that when you were trying to distract that guy?"

I gave her a long look. I wanted to argue with her, but I knew she was right. It had been a dumb thing to do.

"It happened so fast," I said. It wasn't quite the same as admitting that I agreed with her.

She sighed. "I'm just glad you're alright. But try not to do anything like that again."

"Yes, mom," I teased.

"Speaking of...have you called your mom? Does *she* know what you've been up to lately?"

I gave her an exasperated look. "No, I haven't." I frowned. "But I need to. I have to talk to her about Stella's place and all of those rabbits." I smiled sweetly at Lilli.

"I actually know something that you don't know."

She raised one manicured eyebrow at me. I hated that she could do that, though it must be an effective tool with her clients.

"I've been offered a job, *and* I've been kissed by a very cute veterinary technician."

I filled Lilli in, first on Garren's kiss and then on Mina Rourke's job offer as she finished making her green goddess salad. We ate as I picked her brain over the pros and cons of accepting the position. Of course, like any good psychologist she made me look at my career options without giving me a definitive answer — because only I would be able to decide what I should do. She didn't, however, have any problem telling me what I should do about Garren.

"Oh, you definitely need to pursue that kiss. Ooh, maybe we can do a double date — me and Drew, and you and Garren!"

"You are insane. The last thing I should be thinking about right now is dating. Is this how you counsel your clients, tell them to pursue spur-of-the-moment relationships while trying to put their lives back together? I need a job right now, not a date."

She shrugged off my criticism. "So. What if the job and the date are in the same place?" She bonked me on the nose with the handle of her fork.

"Now we're playing 'what if'?"

"What if?" she continued, "First, you decide that this mobile library gig is a good career move. Second, you decide that while you're pursuing this career path you may as well get to know the members of your community. And lastly, this event that you're describing as a date would actually be a public relations opportunity? See, it would all be in the name of community service."

"This is about you liking Officer Andrew Turner, isn't it?" I smiled as I stole a crouton from her salad bowl.

"I am simply trying to share my valuable psychological insight with you." she said airily.

She leaned forward and grinned. "But a double date would be fun, De."

CHAPTER TWENTY-ONE

I FOUND OUT FROM DREW when he called to apologize, again, that the guy they arrested wasn't the murderer, but he was involved. It turns out Augustus Davies had gotten a little bit in debt with the wrong people. Paul Baker gave his buddy up for a reduced sentence. He claimed he was only at the store to clear out the safe, but he couldn't find it. I spoke with Mina Rourke about her job offer. The pay wasn't great, but it was comparable to what I had been making and would give me an annual bonus.

I took the job.

And I finally called my mom. After her initial shock and outrage of being told her daughter had been questioned about a murder, she took the rest of my recount of events very well. She admitted knowing about Stella's relationship with Gregory Martin. She said that she couldn't imagine ever thinking the man would do anything so devious as stealing a rabbit, but didn't I feel foolish for not viewing the *whole* DVD the first time and instead jumping to conclusions?

Leave it to my mom to make me feel like a ten-year-old child all over again.

She did say that she was proud of my final handling of the Gregory-Mudd situation.

I guess that's something. Maybe I am ready to grow up and leave my twenties behind me.

When I shared the news about the job offer from Mina Rourke, she thought it was a wonderful opportunity for me.

"Plus, Deana," she said, "this will give you and me time to decide what to do with Stella's estate. You can live there while we figure it out."

"What about Garren and the rabbits? Are we going to keep paying him to help with them?"

"No. That wouldn't be realistic for the long term. But if you're living there, you can take over the day-to-day things and we can work out a short term budget for him to teach you the extra stuff. There are enough funds in Stella's rabbitry account to cover that. What do you think?"

"I think I know nothing about taking care of rabbits, Mom. And I'll be starting a new job, with management responsibilities. I don't know how much time I'm going to have for anything else."

"Oh, it's only a few bunnies, Deana. Let's just try it and see how it goes."

Only a few bunnies?

I've been having a recurring *Star Trek* themed nightmare involving tribbles ever since.

They look suspiciously like rabbits.

Sarsapa-nilla Latte

from The Sparrow Cafe

Espresso - 1 serving

Half & half - 1/4 cup or to taste

Sarsaparilla syrup - 1 ounce

Vanilla - 1/4 teaspoon

White pepper - dash

Steam half & half

Add remaining ingredients.

Top with whipped cream

ACKNOWLEDGMENTS

Stories can be so easy to dream up, but then so difficult to commit to paper (or computer file), and even though most of the writing process is done alone, there are contributions from others that are essential in order to create a finished product.

Thanks to my husband for his constant support and patience. It can't be easy to share a home with someone who is periodically tuning you out in order to imagine and write about a make-believe world. Thanks to my sisters for taking the time to read my drafts and offer edits and opinions, and to the small but mighty writing group I was blessed to become a part of.

This project began as I was dreaming up ways to embrace a farming life after moving to central Pennsylvania. I loved the idea of keeping and caring for animals that could provide fiber for crafts, and angora rabbits seemed more manageable than goats, sheep, or alpacas (I have zero farm experience). I've learned from research that they are still a great deal of work and time, and not something to just jump into overnight. I'm still rolling the farm dream around in my head as I live out some of those musings on paper. While I also made use of the plethora of videos and websites online, and pages and groups found on social media sites, I've only listed the books on the following resources page that I turned to the most for information on rabbits, some specifically for angoras, but I thank the entire 'cottage industry' rabbit community for all of the work and commitment that they put into caring for these creatures.

RABBIT RESOURCES

ARBA OFFICIAL GUIDE to Raising Better Rabbits & Cavies. American Rabbit Breeders
Association, Inc., 2020.

Completely Angora, 2nd Ed. Kilfoyle, Sharon and Samson, Leslie B. Samson Angoras, 1992.

How to Raise Rabbits. Johnson, Daniel and Johnson, Samantha. Quarto Publishing Group USA Inc., 2019.

The Nervous New Owner's Guide to Angora Rabbits. Sugrue, Suzie. Hare and There
Productions, 2011.

Storey's Guide to Raising Rabbits, 5th Ed. Bennett, Bob. Storey Publishing, 2018.

Don't miss out!

Visit the website below and you can sign up to receive emails whenever Michelle Lorette publishes a new book. There's no charge and no obligation.

https://books2read.com/r/B-A-LWCBB-GLSID

Connecting independent readers to independent writers.

Did you love *Seduced by the Blues*? Then you should read *Blue Collar Wooler* by Michelle Lorette!

Life has changed for Deana Weber. Laid off from her city library job, she has moved to the quaint village of Fox Cove, in central Pennsylvania, where she is now living in a charming Georgian style cottage, has a new job, and also has a garden shed full of angora rabbits. Of course, her new life comes with a few challenges. Besides the dozen rabbits in her inexperienced care, she also has to manage the installation and opening of the new village mobile library and try to navigate her way through a budding romance.

For a young woman on the brink of turning thirty, who is just trying to cope with a nine-to-five work day, Deana is learning that long-term commitments that require her to step out of her comfort zone may be the hardest work of all.

To top it all off, there's also the mystery of a woman lying near death outside of her new library!

It would seem that a librarian's work is never quite done.
COMING SPRING 2025

About the Author

Michelle Lorette lives in central Pennsylvania with her husband, where she works part-time among her first love — books. When she's not writing, you can find her pursuing other crafts and hobbies, traveling, and daydreaming.